COURTSHIP OF THE RECLUSE

Linda Louise Rigsbee

ISBN: 1502539748
ISBN-13: 978-1502539748

DEDICATION

I dedicate this book to my mother.
No one knows better than a parent how difficult it
is to convince the inexperienced that it is easy
to be persuaded into something they think
they would never do.

PROLOGUE

Russell Cade rode his horse to the top of the ridge and stopped, gazing down at the valley below. It had been a long winter, but the valley was beginning to show a little green. Winter wasn't over yet, though, and there would likely be at least one more snowfall. His small herd of Angus cattle was still in the south pasture where they had the protection of a pole barn. The grass in the valley needed to grow a little longer before he brought them here.

He turned the horse and rode back down the hill. It was Friday and he wanted to talk to that girl at the restaurant...Cynthia. He'd been thinking about what he wanted to say for weeks. He had no idea what her wages were and he didn't want to insult her with wages that were too low, but he had figured out what it was worth to him. What he needed was someone to take care of the house while he was working the ranch. It wouldn't cost that much more for two people to eat than one, and he had plenty of room for a live-in maid. He had thought to get an older woman, but ever since he had been going to the restaurant, Cynthia had been on his mind. She was personable and professional. She seemed more mature than the others...not given to inane giggling and gossip. She treated him with respect, never participating in the behind-the-hand snickering that the others did.

He was well aware that he was an abnormal sort...and equally aware that he wasn't going to change. It had been three years since he came home and found his mother dead in her room. He had been aware that she was miserable alone in that big house. She had grown up in a large house with nice things and lots of parties. His father, her first husband, had tolerated her insatiable desire for socializing almost thirteen years, but ultimately it led to divorce. It had occurred to him many times she never really loved his father. Whether she had finally found true love or simply matured, she seemed to be content at the ranch when Mr. Cade was alive. Russ had good memories of those days. He loved everything about the new set-up, including his step-father. The solitude of the wild beautiful country suited his temperament more than the city had. He enjoyed working with Mr. Cade on the ranch. When Mr. Cade died of a sudden heart attack, Russ had grieved the loss every bit as much as his half-siblings. He had been happy the day he was adopted and was still proud to wear the name Cade. His step-sisters and brothers had not warmed to him, though. It was something he learned to accept. He buried himself in school and the ranch, further alienating them. They all married and left the ranch with no intent to return, but he had stayed, helping Mr. Cade until his death. His mother inherited the ranch and a modest income until her death. She left the ranch to him. The others didn't want the ranch, but they resented the fact that he ultimately inherited what belonged to *their* father.

At the barn, Cade unsaddled his horse and rubbed him down. He gave him some hay and headed for the house. There he bathed and dressed. A trip through the house assured him that everything was in order, so he headed to town for a meal and a night out. It wasn't something he looked forward to in the beginning. It was something he felt he needed to do. Already people referred to him as a hermit. It wasn't that he didn't like people. He simply preferred the open range to an office. Granted, since his mother's death he had pretty much severed contact with the rest of the world. Grief and guilt had haunted him long enough, though. It was time to rejoin civilization, even if it was only in the form of a meal at the diner once a week. It wasn't something he wanted to do...not at first. Each time Cynthia came to his table with a bright smile and spoke to him, he warmed a little more to the idea. After a while he began to entertain the idea of a maid in his home. It would be nice to come in from the range to a hot meal and a smile. It wouldn't be like his mother, who felt obligated to stay at the ranch. Hired help could leave any time they wanted if they found the place too depressing. He'd even give them the run of the ranch and the loan of a horse to do it. He'd have to find someone who liked that type of thing, though. He wasn't sure why he thought Cynthia was a good fit for the job, but he'd find out before he hired her. He wasn't going to make the job sound like fun. The house was cold and the only form of entertainment was a wall full of books. He had always found them more entertaining than a television. An occasional trip to town to see a movie was all the socializing he could stand for a couple of months. People were up and down the aisles constantly going to the restroom or buying huge buckets of popcorn and candy. Sometimes he wondered whether they came to see the movie or eat. Then there were the parents who dropped their boisterous kids off so they could have an evening alone. Did the kids act that way at home? He'd rather take a long ride through the hills of his three thousand acre ranch. Nothing on that big screen could compare to its beauty, and the quiet country was soothing. He always slept well at night after a long day of work on the range.

He was acutely aware that his taste in entertainment and everything else was out of tune with the rest of the world. Still, he couldn't withdraw from the world. He had seen what it had done to his mother. He wouldn't let himself be drawn into that kind of isolation.

He grabbed the old western hat that had belonged to his step-father from the hook on the wall beside the door. Clamping it on his head, he opened the door. Tonight was like any other chore. It had to be done and it had to start somewhere.

CHAPTER ONE

Cynthia Turley was in the middle of cleaning his favorite table when he walked through the diner door. Something about the lean rancher urged her to reach out to him. Maybe it was the fact that he never smiled, or the loneliness in those green eyes. Whatever the case, she always made sure his table was ready when he arrived. She could set her clock by his arrival - eight o'clock every Friday night - in a blue plaid western shirt and battered black cowboy hat.

His tall frame swayed across the room with feline grace. Removing his hat, he glided into the booth. He glanced up at her; the sun darkened face with its thin lips completely devoid of emotion.

"The usual," he said.

She nodded. He wasn't much for conversation. Other than occasional attempts to draw him out, she respected his privacy. She moved to the counter without writing anything down.

"Steak and Potatoes," she announced to the cook, ignoring the stifled snickers of the other two waitresses. Why they found it so amusing that Mr. Cade was a recluse evaded her comprehension. Right now he was simply a customer.

She poured a cup of coffee and delivered it to him - along with a cheerful smile. "Cold out there, isn't it?"

He shrugged. He never wore a coat and she wondered if he even felt the cold west Texas wind.

She started to walk away, but his adverse response lured her to pause.

"Spring is around the corner."

She smiled again. "It's still two months away, though. I can hardly wait."

He nodded again and turned away, staring out the window while he sipped the coffee. The conversation was over - or so she thought.

When she delivered his meal, he glanced up at her.

"What time do you get off?"

She stared at him. "Nine."

He nodded. "I'd like to talk to you. May I wait here until then?"

She nodded, still regarding him with disbelief. "Of course."

What would he have to talk to her about? If all their conversations in the three months he had been coming to the diner were put together, it was doubtful that they would make a respectable paragraph. On the positive side, at that rate their conversation should be over by five minutes after nine. Then she could walk home in peace. The clattering of dishes, the hectic scramble at lunch, and the incessant gossiping of her coworkers left her at the edge of her patience at the end of the day. That quiet walk home was her chance to relax - that and a good book.

Promptly at nine, she removed her apron and crossed to the table where Cade sat nursing his fifth cup of coffee. She slid into the opposite bench and let her gaze drop significantly to the cup in his hand. "You're not going to sleep a wink tonight."

He stared down at the cup absently. "Never has any effect on me."

Somehow that was no surprise. She waited for him to open the conversation, idly wondering if it would be ten before he spoke. Finally she cleared her throat. "The diner closes at ten."

He glanced up and nodded. "How long have you been working here?"

"Six months - since Dad died. I took care of him for three years - ever since I graduated from high school."

He nodded and fell silent again.

She crossed and uncrossed her legs, studied her fingernails and finally decided to prompt him again. "I understand you have a big ranch west of here."

He gave the usual nod. "Forty miles."

She pursed her lips and whistled softly. "That's a long way to drive for steak and potatoes."

For a second she thought he was going to smile. His eyes flashed with humor, but it was gone before it could reach his lips.

"Do you like working here?" He finally asked.

She shrugged. "The work isn't so bad." When he continued to watch her, she gave him a wry smile. "I'm not much of a social person I guess."

"I see." He was watching her with an intent expression. "You'd be happier taking care of a rambling old house in the middle of nowhere?"

She laughed. "That's not as far out as you might think." She sobered and stared at her hands. "I guess I should go to college and make something of myself. When I was taking care of Dad there wasn't time to take classes and he died owing a lot of money, so I had to sell the house."

Why was she revealing her private affairs to this stranger? She shrugged, her face growing warm. "I guess those are all excuses. I suppose I'm simply not very ambitious."

His brows lifted slightly and his gaze was direct. "What is ambition?"

She stared at him. Surely his vocabulary included such a simple word. "It's ..." She paused, realizing he was looking for a deeper meaning. She shrugged again. "I suppose it is different things for different people - dreams or goals."

He was still watching her intently. "So looking after a rambling old house could be an ambition?"

She squirmed under his penetrating stare. What was this thing he had about an old rambling house? She finally shrugged once more. "I suppose so."

He shifted his attention to the lighted street. Apparently he was merely looking for companionship - his kind. She was beginning to relax when he launched the question.

"Would you be interested in minding my place?"

She gaped at him. "*Your* place?"

He nodded. "It's an heirloom of sorts; a big old house - too much for me to take care of and work the ranch as well." He paused, watching her expectantly. "I don't know what kind of wages you draw here, but I'd be willing to pay you a hundred a week plus room and board."

Slowly the facts were beginning to seep through the layer of shock. He was offering her a job as a live-in maid. The wages weren't all that great, but deducting rent, utilities and groceries from her present salary, it wound up being a good deal more. Basically she would be saving $400 a month instead of $10. Was it merely coincidence that her lease would be up next Friday and the landlord was raising the rent? She gnawed at her lower lip. But staying out there alone with a man?

"Are there neighbors near you?"

He shook his head. "I have over three thousand acres. It's isolated and lonely and I'm gone most of every day. In the winter the landscape is bleak and the house is drafty. The house sits more than a mile off the snow plow route, so sometimes I'm snowed in for a week or so."

She wrinkled her nose. "You make it sound so attractive. How could I refuse?"

He stared at her for a moment. "Are you accepting the job?"

It was hard to tell whether the sarcasm had gone over his head or he simply wasn't amused. She sighed.

"Not yet. What would my duties entail?"

His expression was bland – his voice unemotional, as if he were discussing the weather. "Laundry, dishes - general housekeeping - cooking my meals. I eat breakfast at six in the morning and supper at six in the evening. Sometimes I come in for lunch and sometimes I'd expect you to pack me a lunch. The rest of the time you're free to do as you please. I have some horses you can ride and there are several creeks, ponds and even a small lake on the land."

She rested her elbows on the table and cupped her chin in her hands, staring out into the night. The last sentence was the clincher. Riding horses was one of her favorite pastimes, and the country out that way was gorgeous - winter or summer. Best of all, she could save a substantial amount of money for a down payment on her own place. It all seemed to be tailor made to her preferences - all but the part about staying alone in the house with him. Of course, Mr. Cade hardly seemed the seductive type and she certainly wasn't going to encourage it. Finally she met his patient gaze.

"Let me think about it for a while. Okay?"

His nod was nonchalant. "Fine. I'll be in next Friday. If you decide to take the job, have your things ready then."

He gulped the last of his coffee and stood. "Thanks for your time."

With that he turned and left the diner.

The walk home was quiet, but hardly relaxing. In fact, she was so keyed up when she reached her apartment that she decided to call her best friend with the news.

"Mary? This is Cynthia." She said when a familiar voice answered on the fifth ring. "Hey, you'll never guess what happened tonight."

The voice on the other end of the line responded in a dry tone. "You accepted a date."

"No."

"That's as far out as I can get. What happened?"

"You know that man I was telling you about - the one who comes in at exactly eight every Friday night?"

"The good looking one?"

"I didn't say he was good looking," Cynthia said. "I said he had interesting eyes."

"Yeah, okay - whatever. Did he ask you out?"

"No - well, in a way, I guess. He offered me a job out at his place."

A moment of silence preceded Mary's response. "Let me get this straight. You *are* talking about the guy everyone in town calls the hermit - Russell Cade."

Cynthia grinned. "One and the same. He needs someone to look after his house while he's working the ranch."

After a long pause, Mary's voice sounded concerned. "Cindy, that's forty miles out in the middle of nowhere. Have you seen that house? It looks like something out of a horror movie. Besides, it's huge."

"So he says. No, I haven't seen it, but I won't be driving the forty miles every day, either. He offered me a hundred dollars a week plus room and board."

Mary gasped. "You intend to stay out there - alone with him?"

Cynthia looped the coils of the telephone cord around her finger. "It does sound a little eccentric, doesn't it?"

"Eccentric? It sounds downright scary."

"Oh, he's not mean. He just isn't social. What can you expect out of a recluse?"

"Cindy, I've known Russell Cade since he first moved to this area - since high school. He's as sweet as he can be and I have no doubt his intentions are honorable. But aren't you a little concerned about what people will say? I mean, a pretty young girl living alone with an eccentric bachelor - and what about Russ? Don't you think he might get ideas?"

"You make him sound like an old lecher. Do you know something I don't? As for what the town thinks, I don't care. I didn't grow up around here like you, and I don't intend to spend the rest of my life working at the diner. Not that anyone cares what I do. We're living in the 20th century, Mary - the end of it at that. Anyway, I'm not pretty. In fact, I'm tall, skinny and awkward. My mouth is too big and all teeth."

"You'd put on some weight if you'd slow down a little. You do more work than the other two girls put together. Sure, you're thin, but you've got everything situated right. If he isn't blind or dead, I'm sure he's noticed. As for your mouth, people are always commenting on your beautiful smile and how those blue eyes of yours are so full of life. Are you trying to tell me he hasn't even noticed all that?"

"Don't forget the mess of red hair and freckles. I suppose he missed those. Oh, and you know what they say: Men don't make passes at girls who wear glasses."

"Auburn hair - and you barely have enough freckles for anyone to notice. Don't get on that kick about how ugly you are. I've noticed the guys eyeing you - glasses and all. Now tell me. What else does the hermit want for his $100 a week?"

"Oh for crying out loud, Mary. Don't you think he's a little old for me? Anyway, he's about as romantic as a doorstop. All he wants is a housekeeper."

"Old? Oh yeah. I forgot. He's almost thirty - like me." She sighed. "So you're not the least bit interested in him?"

"Not romantically. If I were, I wouldn't take the job. Do you think I'm crazy?"

"No, just naive."

"Why? Because I'm still looking for a guy who doesn't make me feel like a tease when I won't sleep with him - or because you think I'll never find a man like that?"

"Because I think you just did. I don't know if the years have changed his philosophy, but he used to feel the same way you do. No hanky-panky until after marriage."

"Good for him, but what does that have to do with me working for him? I'd think that would make you even more comfortable with the idea. Or do you think I'm going to lead him astray? Honestly, Mary. It sounds like you've got a case on him. You can have him. All I want is the job."

The line was silent for a few moments. Finally Mary let loose with a heavy sigh. "We're all only human. We can all be tempted. It's fine to have high ideals about not going too far, but the reality of it is, it can happen before you realize what is happening."

"Oh, come on. When you start removing your clothes, naive or not, you've got to realize you're doing something wrong. All it takes is the resolve to stop - provided you actually want to stop."

"Bingo. Maybe you won't want to."

"*With Mr. Cade*?" Cynthia rolled her eyes in exasperation. "You have nothing to worry about. Even if he were a gorgeous stud, I wouldn't become romantically involved with my boss. You know how I feel about that sort of thing."

Mary's tone became dry again. "I know. You've told me a zillion times. But ... Oh, what's the use? Did you call me to get my opinion or to tell me you're going to take the job? It sounds like you've already made up your mind."

"I know. It's just that it sounds so right. You can't imagine how I've missed the country. I hate it in town, and the diner is so...boring. Besides, this way I can save some money. The way things are going now, I'm lucky to save ten dollars a week."

"How many times have I offered to let you stay with me - free? Even if you paid me half my rent, you could still save money."

"I know, and I appreciate your offer. But that's a good way to ruin a terrific friendship. We've been all through this a zillion times."

Silence again.

"Mary?"

"I'm still here. You'd better give this some serious thought. I know you're attracted to him, but..."

"The only thing I'm attracted to is his job offer - and the idea of getting out of this gossipy little town."

"Whatever. Just think it over and don't jump into something you might live to regret."

For the next week Cynthia listened to - and even found herself instigating - discussions about Mr. Cade. When picking up her mail at the post office, she often talked to Adrena. Being the only postal employee in a small town, the petite extrovert was always ready for conversation. She had an opinion about everything – and an uncanny habit of being right.

"Nothing today," Adrena said as Cynthia dug in her purse for the box key.

"Again" Cynthia sighed, abandoning her search. "How are things going today?"

"Same old same old. How about you?"

"Nothing much – as usual."

"You ought to go out once in a while. People are starting to wonder if you don't like them."

Adrena never minced words. Cynthia shrugged.

"You know how I am."

"Yeah," Adrena snickered. "Not much better than the hermit. At least he's coming to town regular now – regular for him."

"He does seem a bit reclusive." Cynthia responded, focusing her attention on a speck of dirt on the counter. "I don't know much about him."

Adrena's laugh was short and humorless. "You haven't missed much."

Cynthia looked up at Adrena. "Do you know him?"

Adrena rolled her eyes. "Nobody knows Russell Cade. Do you remember that rumor in school? Oh yeah, you weren't around here then. I never believed it anyway. I figured his sister started it because she was jealous of him. I guess his stepfather thought more of him than her. After she got married and moved to Colorado the family information stopped – if you know what I mean. He comes in now and then to get things, but don't talk much." Adrena grinned. "Kind of like you."

Cynthia smiled. "Maybe he'd rather listen than talk."

Adrena stamped a letter. "I guess so. From what I hear, he's pretty...frugal; I guess would be the best word. Dependable, though. Mr. Catlin at the bank says he's as honest as they come. The ranchers around here say they can always count on him to help when they're in a bind. Even so, I don't know anyone who admits to understanding him - much less calling him a friend. He's a strange one."

"It sounds like he's a respectable person who likes to keep to himself."

"Yeah." Adrena said, wrinkling her nose. "A regular hermit."

"I guess being reclusive is a poor way to make friends." Cynthia shrugged. "On the other hand, maybe it's a good way to avoid trouble."

Adrena tipped her head to the side and studied Cynthia thoughtfully for a moment. "Is that why you don't date?"

Cynthia's face grew warm. "Maybe so. Men can be a trial sometimes."

"Like your father?" Adrena's gaze was probing.

"That was different. My father couldn't do anything about his health."

Adrena lifted her brows and tossed the letter in a slot. "He could have gone to a nursing home so he wasn't such a burden on his daughter."

"He offered to do that. I wouldn't let him. How could I enjoy myself knowing he was being tended to and surrounded by strangers?"

Adrena nodded. "That sounds like your kind of logic - always thinking of the other person first. Admirable, but you're never going to get anywhere doing that."

"All I want is a small place of my own. Somewhere I can have a garden and maybe a horse. I guess that's my idea of getting somewhere."

"Well, if that's what you want. Go for it. Maybe you could hire on as a nanny at Old Man Taylor's ranch. He's got two boys that...well, calling them a handful would be an understatement. Maybe that's not too good an idea after all." She snickered. "I bet if anyone could straighten them out, it would be you, though."

Cynthia caught her breath. "Geez, is my reputation that bad?"

"Bad? I'd like to have your reputation. Your boss says you're the best thing that ever happened to the diner. The guys think you're..."

"A prude?" Cynthia interjected.

"Conservative would be a good word."

"Dull would be another."

"I wouldn't call you dull, just inactive."

"Well, whatever I am, I'd better get home. It's almost time for you to close. Have a nice evening."

Cynthia left the post office feeling better about Russell Cade than she did about herself. Still, what about the rumor? What could have happened so long ago that people still remembered it? But then, they seemed to remember everything - probably because they kept it revived for entertainment. Where Russell Cade was concerned, the only thing they seemed to have against him was the fact that he provided them no new topics. Good for him.

The conversation with Adrena was comforting, but Mary maintained her viewpoint. She couldn't argue his virtues, but she still insisted that the situation was conducive to trouble. Apparently she found Mr. Cade not only attractive, but also irresistible. Obviously it had been a long time since she had seen or talked to Mr. Cade. That was one facet of the job that didn't trouble Cynthia. Her greatest concern was whether she could manage such a large house on her own. Even the isolation didn't trouble her. Still, there was one question she couldn't ask the townspeople. Why had Cade singled her out for the job? Jennie was the logical choice. The voluptuous brunette was pert and sophisticated. Angie was buxom and plump, but she was a hilarious entertainer. It was a question she'd have to ask Cade.

Everything considered, it was easier to make the decision to take the job than to placate Mary. Eventually Mary accepted the inevitable and even offered the use of an old shed to store everything Cynthia wouldn't take with her. The house was furnished, so she didn't have much to move – just a few pieces of her parent's furniture and some summer clothes. Dad's old truck had been sitting at Mary's since it broke down.

When Mr. Cade strode into the diner Friday night, Cynthia's clothes were packed and stored in the back room of the diner. Chet glanced at her. He had said his peace Wednesday when she gave notice. He liked Cade, but not the situation.

She approached Cade's table hesitantly. What if he had changed his mind? After all, he was a recluse and undoubtedly enjoyed the solitude of a quiet ranch.

His brows lifted when she stopped at his table. "Well?"

She twisted her apron with nervous fingers. "I have my things ready...but I have a few questions first."

He watched her expectantly so she dove in.

"Why me? There are two other waitresses here."

He glanced across the room at Jennie and Angie. "You seem to enjoy your work - and you are respectful toward me."

She considered his response. "I suppose I do enjoy the work, and I try to act respectful to all our customers."

He nodded. "Exactly. Your attitude is professional."

He watched her for a moment and finally lifted his brows again. "You said several."

She smiled. "Your answers were all encompassing."

His nod was brief. "Are you ready to go?"

"My shift doesn't end until nine."

He nodded. "Do you have a car?"

"No. I have a truck, but it hasn't started for a month. I live close enough, so I simply walked. I parked it at a friends' house."

"What's wrong with it?"

"I don't know. One day it wouldn't start. I bought a battery, but it didn't do any good. I was trying to save enough money to get it repaired."

"Well, show me where your things are and I'll take them out to my truck while I wait. Go ahead and order my

17

supper." He stood and stared down at her. "Have you had anything to eat yet?"

"I ate a while ago on my break."

She led him to the back room where her things were piled and resumed her last hour of work at the diner.

CHAPTER TWO

Russell Cade was a meticulous driver. He drove the speed limit...no more; no less. He maneuvered each turn with precision. The dim instrument panel light revealed a strong profile with an aquiline nose and prominent cheekbones. He was by no means a handsome man but his facial features did suggest a stolid character. The years had not been kind to him. He looked closer to forty than thirty. That might be the result of too much exposure to the elements. Apparently he spent a lot of time on the back of a horse, riding his range in all kinds of weather - a fact that prompted more than one comment by townsfolk that he had wasted a good college education. Considering his comment about ambition, he probably didn't consider the education wasted. Obviously he liked ranch work better than anything he had studied.

She shifted in the seat and peered into the night. They must be nearing their destination. Her gaze tried to outrun the headlights and gave up, following the broken line on the highway as it leaped from the dark and shot forward, disappearing under the truck. She rubbed her eyes and tilted her watch crystal around until the light reflected enough to read the dial...ten-thirty. She yawned. This would be one Saturday she wouldn't have to crawl out of bed and get ready to go to the diner. From now on it would be crawl out of bed and cook, clean and then maybe rest a little. What was the house like? Even Mr.

Cade had hinted that it was unusually large. Again she wondered if she had bitten off more than she could chew.

The truck turned off the main road and lurched down a long drive. A structure loomed dark against the lighter horizon. Could that be the house? She held her breath as they approached and turned into the circular drive. As the truck came to a halt in front of the house, she stared up at it in awe. Mary was right. It had an eerie atmosphere, almost as if it were leaning over the truck, investigating the new arrival.

She followed Cade up the steps and across the wide porch, waiting as he unlocked the door. He stepped back to let her enter first. Inside was a spacious foyer sporting a long graceful stairway. To the left was a tall narrow window, bare to the coldness of the room. To their right was a doorway into a huge family room. In one corner a piano perched silently. The embers of a fire still cast a faint glow from a massive fireplace. She shivered, clutching her coat closer. A strong hand gripped her elbow.

"I told you the house was drafty. Here, let me show you where you will sleep."

He led her down a short hallway and opened the first door. Reaching inside the door, he flipped the light switch and the room was flooded with light from a ceiling fan.

"I fixed the door so it locks from the inside." He dug in his pocket and produced two keys still on their original ring. "Here are the keys. That door over there is your personal bathroom." He turned abruptly and left the room.

The sting of his cool hospitality was quickly replaced with awe as she turned back to the room. She gazed at the room in rapt silence. The large room contained some of the most beautiful antique furniture she had ever seen. The wood appeared to be cherry, and although it could use a coat of wax, it still had a deep luster. Instead of a closet, a large wardrobe stood at one end of the room, dwarfing a vanity desk with a large oval mirror. A chest of drawers with copper handles sat beside the bed - and what a bed it was. The carved headboard was beautiful but it was the lace canopy and matching bedspread that caught and held her attention. It was fit for a queen.

"I hope you don't find all this too primitive," Cade spoke behind her.

She swung around and stared at him. "Primitive?"

"The furniture - it was handed down to my mother and she left it to me. It's old, but still in good condition. I recently put a new inner spring mattress on the bed, but the rest of it is exactly as she left it."

"Left it? Did your mother pass away?"

"She died." He answered in a brusque tone as he deposited her things in the middle of the room. "I'll show you around a little before I turn in."

They trekked back down the hallway to the family room and then into a spacious kitchen. The appliances were modern but the cabinets were old and solid. The floor was as clean as the counters. Copper-bottomed cookware hung from hooks on one wall. A small round table and two chairs were placed in a corner near the doorway to the family room, providing a view of the fireplace.

"I eat in here," he said. "I only use the dining room when I have company."

The laundry room was also clean and an old wringer tub still sat in one corner, as though unwilling to completely surrender to modern appliances.

Cade stretched and yawned. "Well, make yourself at home. I'm going to turn in. If you need anything, my room is at the end of the hall. You'll find extra blankets in the entry closet if you need them."

He turned and left the room, his boots clicking across the tile floor and then fading as he moved across the hardwood family room floor and down the hall.

She glanced around the kitchen, knowing she should familiarize herself before breakfast, but feeling uncomfortable about exploring so soon after her arrival. What would he want for breakfast? The best way to decide was to find out what he had in the refrigerator.

She opened the refrigerator - milk, eggs, and bacon - the usual supplies. A little more exploring revealed that the cabinets were stocked with sufficient supplies of dry goods and the potato and onion bins were full. Was there anything Cade didn't do efficiently? The answer came to her so quickly that it brought a smile to her lips. Participate in conversation.

Returning to her designated room, she hung all her clothes in the cedar lined wardrobe and tucked her personals in the spacious dresser. At eleven she finally crawled into the bed. She was exhausted, and morning would arrive all too soon. She set the alarm and fluffed the pillows, but it did no good to close her eyes. They kept popping back open. Her mind was up, wandering the huge house - and Cade's mind. Why had he suddenly decided he needed a maid - or was it sudden? Could there be truth to Mary's suspicions. No. She couldn't believe that there was any thought of romance going on in Cade's mind. He had probably reached a point that the ranch and house were too much work. Seeing her at the diner probably gave him the idea of getting help.

She glanced at the door, realizing she had forgotten to lock it. Not that it mattered. If he intended her harm, he would hardly have fixed the door so it would lock from the inside. Of course, he could have had more keys made - in which case, it wouldn't matter if it was locked or not. She thought of the movie Psycho and immediately wished she had never watched it. The night was cold and she was cozy in the bed. There was no point in freezing her buns off darting across the cold floor to lock the door. Her eyelids drooped and finally she slept.

The alarm clock buzzed insistently and she reached over to slap the snooze button, squinting at the iridescent hands. Five a.m. She threw the covers back and gasped. It was miserably cold in the bedroom. Tossing her gown aside, she hurriedly pulled on some sweats and made the bed. Opening her door quietly she carried her shoes to the kitchen before putting them on. Then she lit the oven and washed her hands.

By the time Cade arrived in the kitchen she had biscuits, gravy, bacon and eggs ready. Cade dropped into a chair and immediately began to put away the food. She poured him a cup of coffee and he glanced up at her.

"Sit down and eat."

"I never eat this early in the morning."

Still, she poured herself a cup of coffee and sat down at the table. "Do you want me to pack you a lunch?"

He shook his head, declining to answer until he had swallowed the food in his mouth.

"I'll be in at twelve."

He sipped his coffee. "Sandwiches will be fine today. Spend some time exploring the house. Make a list of anything you need and I'll drive into town Monday."

Would she be invited along, or would she be expected to stay on the ranch? Always? She sipped her coffee reflectively and finally found the courage ask him a question that had been nagging her since his offer.

"Mr. Cade, do you mind if I have a friend over now and then?"

His head lifted and he frowned at her. "Russ, or Russell. Don't call me Mr. Cade. It makes me feel old."

He swigged the last of his coffee and set the cup in his plate, carefully placing the flatware across the plate before he continued.

"You may call or have friends over anytime you wish...as long as they don't interfere with your work." He

23

pushed his chair back and stood. "I've got to get going. The sun will be up soon." He lifted his hat from a peg on the wall and shrugged into his coat.

"See you at lunch." He said as he walked out the door.

Cynthia finished the dishes and wiped the counters. Last night she had noticed a few clothes in a hamper in the laundry room. As she passed through the living, room she paused and smiled. A fire burned brightly in the fireplace. Cade had been busy this morning.

Removing the laundry from her room, she walked down the hall and hesitated at Cade's bedroom door. Somehow it seemed an invasion of his privacy, but it was part of the job. She turned the porcelain knob and pushed the door open. His room was also filled with antique furniture, although his appeared to be mahogany. The bed was made and she found his clothes in the hamper. The master bath was tidy, so she left the room and pulled the door shut, breathing a long sigh.

With the laundry washing and the sun peeping through curtainless panes, she set out to explore the house. First she opened the double doors in the kitchen and found the formal dining room. A long oak table graced the center of the room, its ten carved chairs at attention. A matching china cabinet held fine china, crystal and silverware. The silverware needed polishing and the furniture could use a good dusting. She closed the doors when she left the room, anticipation increasing her pulse. It was such an interesting house.

The long curving stairway invited and she ascended to the second floor. The landing paused at the Y of two long hallways. The floor creaked as she chose the one on the right. Three empty bedrooms were closed off to the heat, as well as a full bath that looked as though it hadn't been used in years. Apparently the water had been shut off up here to keep it from freezing. Retracing her steps, she advanced down the second hallway. Another full bath and two more bedrooms - all empty. As she glanced into the last bedroom, she noticed it had a patio door. Closer investigation revealed a balcony that overlooked the driveway. This room also had a fireplace and a door adjoining the bathroom. She ran her fingers along the smooth marble mantle. What a beautiful room - and empty. Even as the idea occurred that she would rather have this room, she knew she couldn't ask. He had made his choice - suggesting something else would be rude. Still, the rich hardwood floor reflected the weak morning sun in a cheerful manner that spawned reluctance to continue the tour. This would be a good place to come to relax, though - when the weather warmed. She rubbed her arms and left the room.

At the end of the hall, a steep set of stairs led to the attic. The stairs groaned as she climbed and the door squealed as she opened it. A small frosted window allowed light to enter the room that was obviously a storage space for heirlooms. A spinning wheel stood in one corner, partially covered by a dusty sheet, and beside it, a mahogany rocker with a cobbler seat. There was an old treadle sewing machine with carved drawers and even a grandfathers' clock, stating the permanent time of three p.m. Imagine the stories that must lurk in the walls of this house. A large chest invited, and she knelt, touching the lid. Something private - or more interesting antiques? She lifted the lid. Inside were tiny sweaters and booties. Each set was carefully sealed in a clear zipper bag. They looked unused...his mothers' hobby, or was there a sad story? She closed the lid and ran her fingers across the dull copper latch. It was dusty. This was one place Cade obviously didn't spend much time. She stood and glanced around the room again. Such beautiful things should be displayed in the rooms downstairs. The grandfather clock would look beautiful in the foyer, and the rocker should be in the living room, near the piano. She sighed and left the room, carefully pulling the door shut.

As she descended the long stairway again, her palm caressed the smooth dark wood of the banisters. It was such a beautiful house - and so cold. She rubbed her arms again and headed for the living room, which was now comfortable. The fire was burning down, though, so she added more wood. She stared into the flames, wondering why none of the windows had curtains, and why so many things were left to gather dust in the attic. The floor was cold. Why no rugs? She curled up on the couch and fell asleep.

Waking with a start, she glanced at her watch. Fifteen minutes until twelve. She leaped from the couch and darted into the kitchen. Her first day and she had fallen asleep on the job. Working as fast as she could, she started a pot of coffee and sliced some ham. As she completed setting the table, the screen door squealed and Cade opened the door. He stomped his boots and shook white flakes from his hat and coat before entering the house

Cynthia poured them both a cup of coffee as he washed at the sink.

"How long has it been snowing?" She asked.

He dried his hands with the towel. "It just started. It looks like it might get bad. Do you have a list yet?"

She blushed. "No, I'm afraid I didn't get around to it yet."

He noted her rising color and shrugged. "No problem. I don't think we need much of anything." He dropped to a chair and built himself a sandwich. "Did you call your friend yet?"

"No. I didn't...I thought...It's long distance, you know."

He shrugged again without looking up. "Keep in touch with people. It gets lonely out here."

He should know. Which came first, the recluse or the loneliness? She set the coffeepot back on the stove.

"Are you lonely?"

"No." He took a bite of his sandwich and washed it down with coffee.

She fashioned a sandwich. "Was your mother lonely?"

He glanced up at her, and his mouth twitched. "Yes."

"What happened to her?"

He swallowed his food. "Eat your lunch." His attention was back on his food.

Her face felt hot and cold by turns. His cool reproach smarted, but the previous terse answers about his mother should have warned her that it was a touchy subject.

At any rate, he was a recluse and he probably didn't want a babbling female around. She took a bite of her sandwich and glanced up when he finally spoke, his tone brusque.

"She died of a broken heart. I thought everybody around here knew about the Cade's."

"I'm not from around here. I grew up thirty miles to the north." She paused and her voice took on a sardonic tone. "Where Cade wasn't a household word," she concluded.

He glanced up sharply, his gaze searching her face.

She stood, picking up a plate. "I apologize for badgering you about your mother. I didn't realize you were so sensitive about it."

"I'm not sensitive." The words were curt.

In spite of her irritation, she couldn't help smiling. Actually there was nothing sensitive about Russell Cade. He was merely a private person - private and unsociable. She knew that when she accepted the job so any complaint at this point would be out of line.

She shrugged. "No, I suppose not."

He watched her intently for a few moments longer and then turned his attention to his food. How he did it, she couldn't say, but when he finished his meal, not even a crumb was left on the plate.

He strode to the door, clamped on his hat, shrugged into his coat and left the house without so much as a good-bye. She watched him head for the barn and wondered how he could stand being out in the cold all day. He was probably used to it. The snow was coming down in big heavy flakes now. She rubbed her arms again. Why didn't he do something about this cold house? But he had warned her about the cold - warned her about the snow. Would they be snowed in for a week now? No point mulling over a decision she had already made. The best way to beat the cold was to work up some heat. The first thing she needed to do was the dishes. Then make that list.

An hour later she found herself staring vacantly into the fire again. She shook her head free of pointless thoughts and began dusting. There was enough to do around here and she intended to earn her pay - without supervision. First she dusted the dining room and polished the silverware. Then she began cleaning the family room. Carrying a chair from the kitchen, she stretched to dust the top shelf of one of the bookcases beside the fireplace. A large green book caught her attention. The Lonely Hills, by Elizabeth Cade. She removed the book from the shelf and opened it to the dedication page. "To my only friend, Russell Cade." His mother or his wife? She leafed through the book, looking for a clue.

The screen door squeaked and the kitchen floor complained as someone crossed it. Cade? She stared at the kitchen doorway, waiting breathlessly for the person to appear. When Cade finally stepped through the doorway holding a cup of coffee, her breath escaped in a long sigh.

"I wasn't sure who came in."

She lifted the book to replace it and he noticed the cover.

"Were you reading that?"

Her face felt hot again. "No...Well, yes. I glanced through it." Was he angry?

He eyed her sardonically. "You're welcome to read anything in the house. It isn't necessary to cover up your interest."

She shoved the book back into its place and gave the shelf a last swipe, curbing her tongue as she dismounted the chair. She lifted the chair and ignored his offer to carry it to the kitchen for her. He was outspoken and direct, but why did it sound so much like he had caught her in a lie?

He followed her to the kitchen. "Are you angry with me?"

She scooted the chair under the table and tossed the rag in the hamper. "Does it matter? I'm here to do a job."

He was quiet long enough to rouse her interest, and she glanced up to determine the cause of his silence. He was lounging against the kitchen doorway, staring down into his coffee cup. Finally he glanced up and met her gaze.

"It matters."

She turned and rested her hands on the back of one of the kitchen chairs.

"Look, Mr. Cade."

"Russ," he interrupted irritably.

She lifted her palms in resignation. "All right, Russ. All you have to do is lay down the ground rules. If you don't want to talk about your mother, we won't. But if I'm supposed to avoid the subject, don't act like I'm in the middle of some deceitful act when I try."

He was clearly surprised. "What makes you think the topic of my mother is..." He stopped mid-sentence and shrugged in resignation. He strode across the room and poured his coffee in the sink. "All right. It's a subject I'd rather not discuss. Not because she did anything wrong, though. I hold myself responsible for her death."

The statement was an open invitation but she was several conversations wiser now, and waited for him to volunteer the rest of the story. He obviously considered the subject closed and remained silent. So on to something else.

"The book I was holding. Did your mother write it?"

He nodded. "That and a couple dozen others. She had a short career as a writer." He rinsed his cup and turned from the sink. As he strode across the room she chanced a last remark.

"I'll try not to be so inquisitive."

He stopped and turned, frowning down at her.

"There's no harm in a healthy curiosity. It's flapping jaws that get people into trouble."

She stared at him. "Do you think my jaws flap too much?"

His expression became sour. "I can get into enough trouble without people squeezing imaginary insults out of my words." He turned and headed for the family room door again. "I'm going to take a warm shower. Do you think you could scare us up a warm snack?" He didn't wait for an answer.

She glanced at her watch. It was three pm. A warm snack? What kind of snack could she whip up in fifteen minutes? She mused through the kitchen cabinets, her attention settling on the can of cocoa. That would do, but what about something to eat with it. Maybe her favorite would work. It was worth a try. She turned on the broiler and buttered some bread.

When Cade came into the kitchen she placed a cup of hot chocolate and a saucer of cinnamon toast before him. He quirked a brow.

"An interesting combination. Smells delicious."

She smiled. "I hope you like it. It always hits the spot for me on cold days."

He tasted the toast and nodded approvingly. "One thing you should know." He glanced up at her. "I don't think you could find anything I wouldn't like. I enjoy variety and I'm not afraid to try anything new, so just cook what you like."

They finished the snack in silence. Afterward he took a book from the shelf and retired to his room. The living room floor could use a mopping and then it would be time to start supper. A glance out the window revealed that the snow had piled up to four or five inches. Was Cade weathering out the storm? The wood box was looking skimpy. Where did he keep the rest of the wood? She wandered through the house, peering out the window until she spotted a small shed. That was probably it. Donning a heavy coat and some rubber boots that she found in the entry closet, she battled the storm to the shed. Opening the door, she found her assumption correct. The shed was piled high with wood. She leaned over and picked up a block of wood.

A yellow ball of hissing fur flew past her. She dropped the wood and screamed before she realized it was only a young cat. She stumbled to the door. "Here kitty kitty."

But the cat had no intention of coming near her. "Are you hungry?" She called to him as he hunkered down beside a rose bush with a few brown leaves clinging to it. He stared at her suspiciously.

She shrugged and went back for an armload of wood. Had the cat been locked in the shed, or had he found a way through the old walls? She piled one arm high and closed the door. If he couldn't get in the shed, he'd probably find some other place to stay warm. She crunched through the snow back to the house and removed her coat and boots before entering the living room.

Cade leaped from the couch as she entered. "Here. I'll get that." He took the wood from her arms and dropped it into the wood box. "You don't need to be carrying heavy things and getting out in this weather. I'll do it."

"It's all right. I enjoyed the fresh air and I even found a potential friend. Did you know you have a cat in the wood shed?"

He made a face. "He comes in through a hole in the floor. I guess I'll have to put something over it. The offspring of some stray, I guess."

"Well, at least you won't have mice in the woodshed."

She watched as he added more wood to the fire and stirred the coals up with the poker. "Do you ever feed him?"

Another sour look. "You start that and he'll hang around for sure."

She dropped to the floor in front of the fireplace and crossed her legs. "I take it you don't like cats."

He squatted beside the fire. "I take it you do."

She shrugged. "It's your ranch. If you don't want me to feed it, all you have to do is say so."

He jabbed at the fire a few times. "I don't care. If you think he'll make good company, go ahead and feed him." He stood and returned the poker to its holder. "Just don't try to tame any of those black kitties with the white stripes down their backs."

She stared up at him. He was obviously making a joke, but she would never have guessed it from the expression on his face. He looked so tall, standing over her that way. She shifted her attention to the fire and rubbed the beginnings of a crick from her neck. Working for Cade might not be as dull as she had first thought.

Linda Louise Rigsbee

CHAPTER THREE

In the next month, her schedule became routine. Once the floors had been waxed and the furniture polished, the house sparkled - in an empty kind of way. The work was rewarding, though, as the house began to take on a homey atmosphere. If only there were some curtains on the windows and rugs on the floors.

The house wasn't the only thing changing, though. Both occupants were gaining a healthy glow...and gaining was the operative word. Cade had put on enough weight to take the hollows out of his cheeks, making him look a good ten years younger. As for Cynthia, her cheeks weren't the only things filling out. All her dresses now fit snugly across the bust, and even her skinny legs were beginning to have some attractive curves. Some of the money she had saved would have to go into new clothing - and soon.

Cade was slowly emerging from his shell, but the cat was still as wild as ever. Scraps from the table coaxed him out even during the daylight hours - but only when she stepped back into the house. She watched from the family room window as he wolfed the food - a habit that had prompted Cade to dub him Scruffy. It was another indication of that underlying humor. If only he would smile with something besides his eyes.

The weather grew intermittently warmer and on one of those sunny warm days, Cade invited her to pack a lunch and join him in a ride on the ranch. The idea was especially welcome, as she had become so organized that cleaning took no more than half the day.

Cade selected a bay mare for her and then reluctantly surrendered the duty of saddling. When Cynthia finished tightening the cinch and lowered the stirrup, she turned to find him watching her. His eyes expressed approval and the thin lips twitched in what she had grown to accept as a smile - fleeting as it was. She wrinkled her nose at him.

"I know. I'm slow."

"The job is done - and done correctly."

That was as close to praise as she was likely to get from him and she smiled her appreciation. Tucking a toe in the stirrup, she swung up into the saddle. Cade mounted a gray gelding and they headed out across the treeless hills.

After nearly an hour of riding, they descended the steep walls of a draw and followed it to a small valley. Protected from the harsh winter storms, the valley was already lush and green. The valley was speckled with healthy Angus cattle. Here and there, calves frolicked with each other, kicking their heels in the air and bellowing their delight at the balmy weather. The adults ignored them, grazing contentedly on the deep grass.

They rode through the herd, which paid little attention to their passage. The animals were sleek and their black fur shone in the sunlight. Cynthia leaned over as they drew near one and tried to pet it, but the cow moved away a few steps and began grazing again. She glanced up to find Cade watching her. His pupils were contracted by the bright sunlight and his light green eyes contrasted sharply with his bronze tan. At that moment he was surprisingly attractive.

She smiled at him. "I guess they're not as tame as they look."

He shrugged. "I'm the only human they see most of the time, and I represent no harm to them. This is the herd I've been developing for about five years. I started with a few select cows and a good bull. I replaced the bull last year to prevent inbreeding, but I've been pleased with the offspring."

"They're beautiful. I don't know what traits you look for in beef cattle, but they look healthy."

He nodded. "They are, and hardy." He turned his horse and started through the herd. "Come on. I want to show you something."

She followed him across the valley and up a steep slope. The inside of her legs were so sore that walking might be more comfortable. He probably didn't realize she wasn't used to riding.

They rode across a mesa and descended to a wide creek. The grass around the creek was new, giving it a velvety look. The creek was clear and swift. When they paused on the bank, she could stand the pain no longer. Leaning into one stirrup, she forced her other leg over the back of the horse and dismounted. Her legs were so numb that she staggered and grabbed the stirrup. The horse snorted and sidestepped, letting her fall to the ground.

Instantly Cade was beside her, helping her up. "Why didn't you say you were tired? We could have stopped any time."

Her face was hot as she pushed away from him, avoiding his gaze. What a pansy he must think she was.

"I'm all right. I'm just a little stiff."

Actually, her legs felt like stumps and her groin muscles were knotted with pain. She hobbled to the edge of the creek. The surface of the water ruptured, spewing a colorful fish into the air. The fish flipped and dived back into the water. Cynthia gasped. Did you see that?" she asked breathlessly. It looked like a Rainbow Trout. She leaned forward, examining the lurking figures under the surface. "There are lots of them. Do you ever fish here?"

He shook his head. "I'm not much of a fisherman."

"Oh, I'd love to come here and fish sometime. Would you mind?"

He gazed down the creek, his expression unreadable. "As long as you eat what you catch. I don't believe in catch-and-release except if the fish is simply too small. We Americans have a nasty habit of playing with our food - like a cat. If you hunt, it should be for food, not pleasure."

She couldn't agree with him more, but it was an unusual viewpoint for a man. She stretched and walked around, gradually gaining feeling in her legs. That might have been a mistake. Every muscle complained so painfully that she wished the numbness would return. She tried to work the muscles in her lower back with her fingertips, but the effort was worse than the benefit.

Suddenly strong fingers began working her shoulder muscles, delightfully descending to the muscles on either side of her spine. She moaned.

"Oh, that feels so good. You can't imagine how sore I am."

"Do you want to go back?"

"How long have we been out?"

"About three hours."

Three more hours back? How could she endure the ride? She tried to smile cheerfully as she looked at him over one shoulder. "Aren't you getting hungry? I'll be fine after we rest for a little bit."

"Sure." The fingers ceased their massage and he took her arm, leading her to a dry rock. "Why don't you rest here a few minutes and I'll do the serving for once."

"But I can..."

His hand pressed down on her shoulder. "So can I. I got along before I hired you and I think I can manage one meal now."

She stretched out on the rock, its warmth penetrating her shirt and further relaxing her muscles. Closing her eyes against the bright sunlight, she absorbed its warmth. She breathed deeply of the clear air and listened to the sound of the creek darting over rocks - swirling against its banks. Somewhere in the distance, a Meadowlark called, its melodic song adding sweetness to the smell of wild roses. It was spring again - at last.

"Are you asleep?"

She opened her eyes and squinted up at him through the sunlight. Languidly lifting a hand, she shaded her eyes and smiled at him.

"No. I'm enjoying this immensely, though." She took the sandwich he offered and grinned. "Is this what you do out here all day long?"

The lips twitched and a brow quirked. "Do you want to swap jobs?"

She laughed. "Only if this is all I have to do."

He squatted beside her and scanned the horizon soberly. "If you figure out a way to do this all day and still make the ranch turn a profit, you could make a fortune teaching your method at seminars."

She sat up and glanced around at the magnificent scenery. "I know the work is hard and the weather is forbidding at times, but do you know how lucky you are?"

He stared at her intently while he chewed a mouthful of food. Finally he swallowed and nodded.

"I know, but there are a lot of people who don't understand."

She crossed her legs painfully and stared down at her sandwich. "Different strokes for different folks," she quipped, and took a bite of the sandwich.

They ate in silence then, enjoying the tranquility of Mother Nature's work around them. Tomorrow would be another day at the house, and she intended to enjoy every minute of this day with Cade. He made an excellent companion, a fact that hadn't occurred to her before that moment. Who would have thought it? Certainly she wouldn't have on the day he offered her the job. But then, a lot of things had changed since that day.

He stood and walked to the edge of the creek, stooping to wash his hands. He was so meticulous - so thoroughly masculine and sexy. She stared down at her sandwich, shocked that the thought had crossed her mind. Cade...sexy? Yet there was something about the way he moved, so full of grace and power. Animal magnetism. That was it - nothing more.

She finished her sandwich and drank some coffee, shoving the thought to the deepest recesses of her mind. Cade was her boss, and thinking such things was not only disrespectful of him, but job threatening as well - especially if he suspected the existence of such thoughts.

Lunch finished, they mounted and started back to the house. The country was beautiful, poised on the edge of spring. A crisp wind caught up with them on the plateau, where not even a tree hindered its progress. She unfolded her jacket collar and hunkered down in the saddle, cold and miserable.

Cade reined in and pointed. Her gaze followed in the direction he indicated. About two hundred yards away a lone wolf stood poised for flight, watching them cautiously. Its legs were long and lean and its head was held low, ears erect. It looked hungry and cold. Cynthia glanced up at Cade.

"Do you lose many cattle to wolves?"

He shrugged. "It's hard to say. I lose some cattle every year. Usually they succumb to the cold, heat or disease, but sometimes they simply disappear. Most of the losses are calves, though. There again, it's hard to say whether they die from natural causes or attacks by predators. Of course, that includes Pumas and coyotes as well."

The wolf finally decided they were no threat and turned his back on them, trotting away across the vast grassland.

"I noticed that you always carry a rifle when you go out. Do you ever shoot any wolves?"

He scowled at her. "The rifle is for emergencies only. I try to live in harmony with nature." He watched the wolf disappear into the tall grass. "The fact is, when wolves attack a herd, they always take the weakest animal. That's the natural selection process at work - survival of the fittest. Farmers don't butcher their best animals, either. They leave them for breeding purposes. It's the hunter that throws nature out of balance, selecting only the best game."

"So you're against hunters and fishermen?"

He glanced at her and his lip twitched. "No, I simply think there is a proper way to do things, and humans have a habit of doing what pleases them at the moment, not what is best for the future."

"So you're saying the wolves improve your herd by culling out the weakest animals?"

Again the lip twitched. "In a manner of speaking. Of course, it would be more profitable for the ranch if I culled those animals by taking them to the slaughter house."

"That's why the other ranchers want to kill off the wolf? To improve their profits?"

"More likely so they can stay in the black. I have enough acreage and cattle to absorb some of the loss. Most of the ranchers are barely getting along as it is." He grimaced. "The trouble is; my ranch has been a safe haven and even headquarters for the wolf population around here. So far I don't think I have a problem, but I have to consider those other ranchers when I decide how many wolves this land can support. The more they get to eat, the more offspring they will produce, and some of those offspring will need to stake out new territory. So far, deer and rabbits are easier for a few wolves to pull down than a healthy cow, but if the pack gets too big they may go after cattle. I don't make the decisions alone, though. State game officials are involved as well." He turned his horse and they started out again.

She hugged her arms and hunched down into her jacket, her teeth chattering. The more she learned about the way he thought, the more she was convinced that people around him were the strange ones, not Cade.

The next time she talked to Mary, she said as much. Mary smiled knowingly.

"I told you so."

"Told me what?"

"You'd fall for him."

Cynthia caught her breath. "I haven't fallen for him. I was simply stating that I agree with the man."

"Sure, and you haven't entertained a single romantic thought about him?" Mary watched her intently.

Cynthia knew her face was getting red. She could feel the warmth of the blush as it crawled up her neck. She rolled her eyes. "Don't be silly. He's a good eight years older than I am."

"Six, but who's counting? Oh, I forgot. You were the one who thought about it long enough to calculate it out." Mary smiled; a devilish twinkle in her eye.

The blush was developing into a burning flame. "Nothing is going on, if that's what you're getting at."

Mary shrugged. "Not yet, anyway."

Cynthia winced. "Don't you have any faith in me at all?"

Mary gnawed on her lower lip and it was her turn to blush. "I'm sorry. I guess I'm judging you by what I'd be doing in your shoes. I had an awful crush on him when we were in high school. He was the one that kept me honest. I sure didn't have that much will power."

Cynthia sighed. "I thought you were mighty interested in him. I should have known. Well, he isn't interested in me, so the door is still open for you."

Mary studied her reflectively and finally spoke in a hushed tone, as if she didn't actually want to know the answer to her question.

"You say he's not interested in you. Are you interested in him?"

The blood bounded back into her neck. "Only as a friend."

Mary smiled and the twinkle came back into her eyes. "Now he's a friend. Before that he was a boss. What will it be a month from now? Don't try to fool an old fool. I can tell by the color in your cheeks. You're falling for him."

"I am not," she snapped and then shrugged. "Let's not argue about it."

Mary raised her brows and then nodded. "All right, let's talk about something else. How is it going with Scruffy?"

Thankful for the change of subject, Cynthia launched into a description of her latest conquests with the cat, again tucking that nagging doubt to the back of her mind. Thinking about Cade in that way could lead to no good. She was simply lonely out there and he was good company - the only company.

CHAPTER FOUR

Gradually winter released its grip and flowers erupted from the ground in celebration of spring. Even Scruffy seemed to acknowledge its arrival, allowing Cynthia to remain on the porch when he ate the table scraps. Eventually her attempts to tame him paid off, and he allowed her to touch him - provided she was careful not to move too quickly. Not unlike another male on the ranch.

Cade was trying to be accommodating, but sometimes he was as skittish about conversation as the cat was about being touched - and likely for the same reason. Neither of them had a clue what was on her mind. In Cade's case, that was probably a blessing at times. Hopefully he had no idea how her heart beat double time occasionally at the strangest things. Like the way his broad shoulders swayed so gracefully with each step as he strode to the corral - or the way he lounged in a doorway, coffee in one hand, one long leg thrown carelessly over the other. And lately her curiosity had been going beyond the usual questions about his mysterious family tree - beyond the questing of his vast knowledge of the ranch. Was it normal to have sudden flashing questions like...what would it be like to kiss him? Was it simply loneliness? Most important, did he ever suspect her foolish thoughts? If he did, he gave no indication. Although at times she caught him watching her thoughtfully. Thankfully it had never been one of the times that she was thinking about him though. Otherwise her expression might have revealed her torrid thoughts. She sighed and wandered through the spotless kitchen. She needed something else to do - something creative. She paused in the kitchen doorway, envisioning the family room redecorated. It wasn't the first time she had done so, but this morning she had run across some curtains and rugs in the attic. Should she ask him about putting them up? So far she had never mentioned her excursions to the attic, but when things got too dull around the house, she went up to explore. The discovery of a second room in the attic had provided more hours of entertainment.

The radio was playing a waltz as she walked through the family room and she moved to the sway of it, dancing with an imaginary friend. She stopped, suddenly aware that Cade was propped against the kitchen door jam, nursing a cup of coffee. Warmth invaded her cheeks and she giggled nervously.

"Don't just stand there. Come join me in a dance. This other guy keeps stepping on my toes."

"I don't do floors," he answered dryly.

She laughed at his dry humor. "You mean you don't know how to dance."

He shook his head soberly. "No reason to learn. I'd rather not make a fool out of myself." He turned and disappeared into the kitchen.

She snapped the radio off. Was he trying to tell her she was acting like a fool? Well, it must have looked that way. She shook her head. Supper was ready and he was probably hungry. But when she came into the kitchen he was nowhere in sight. She pulled the roast from the oven. The carrots and potatoes packed around it were the perfect consistency. She set the table and glanced up when the screen door squeaked.

He didn't wear a coat today and his shirtsleeves were rolled up to reveal brown muscular forearms. The heart thing happened again and she busied herself at the table.

He crossed to the sink. "I'm starved."

"It's ready when you are." She kept her face averted until the warmth left her cheeks. "I still don't know how you can stand that cold wind."

He dropped into his chair. "It feels warm today, but I always keep a light jacket in my saddle bags. I need it when I get in the high country." He accepted the platter of food and heaped his plate. They ate in silence until he finally turned a concerned gaze on her. "Is something on your mind?"

Her cheeks flushed again and in her desperate search for something to explain her preoccupation, she plunged into the subject of the curtains. "You know, this house wouldn't be as cold if there were some curtains on the window and some rugs on the floor."

He took a sip of coffee before responding. "Curtains shut out the light. This place is dark enough as it is." He took a bite of food and watched her intently. Finally he swallowed and spoke. "Does the cold bother you that much?"

"Sometimes. Anyway, it's the paneling that makes the room so dark, not the curtains over the windows. If you use the right colors, and brighten the walls with a few large pictures, or some mirrors, it wouldn't be so dark. The house could use a little cheerful decorating."

For a minute she was afraid she had stepped over the line. He stared at her and frowned. Finally he spoke.

"You think the atmosphere in this house is depressing?"

"Don't you?" Surely he must have noticed.

He gave his attention to the food in his plate. Was he angry? It was hard to tell. Either she had never seen him angry or he had cleverly concealed it - like every other emotion. Finally he finished his meal and scooted his chair back.

"Is that apple pie I smell?"

Why did he do that every time he disagreed with her? She scooted her chair back without responding and went to the laundry room where the pie was cooling. As she re-entered the kitchen, he watched her cross to the table. He rubbed his jaw reflectively.

"There are some curtains and rugs in the attic - I'm sure you've already found them. If you want to put them up, go ahead. I don't spend that much time in the house anyway."

She sliced the pie absently. "What makes you think I found them?"

He gave her a sour look. "Don't toy with my mind. Anyone as bright and curious as you would have to explore that attic. Now cut me a piece of that pie."

Warmth flooded her neck and crawled up her cheeks. It was bad enough to be caught snooping in his things, but being accused of deception as well - and for the second time. She cut a piece of the pie and served it to him on a clean saucer. Did he really think she was bright? Handing out compliments seemed to be out of character for him, but hadn't he always been honest and direct?

She sat down with a piece of pie and poked at it. "I noticed some crocus and daffodils coming up in the front. It's almost spring."

He never looked up from his food. "Do you like flowers?"

She laughed softly. "Does a dog have ears?"

He glanced up at her laugh and watched her intently. What was he thinking when he did that? Finally he shrugged. "Down in the lower pastures there are already some flowers in bloom. If you'd like, I'll bring a few home sometime."

She blushed again. "That would be nice." To him it was nothing more than bringing home a gallon of milk or a sack of feed. Yet it was touching and somehow personal. The darkening shadows sharpened his features and highlighted the crows' feet around his eyes. He finished his pie and leaned back in his chair, his gaze meeting hers. She knew the color was deepening in her cheeks.

He watched her thoughtfully, running a hand across his mouth absently. "You know, that family room could use a woman's touch."

She jumped at the diversion. "It needs something light and not too distracting from the natural beauty of the room - something that would complement the antique quality."

He nodded. "It has a lot of character." He leaned back and gazed into the room. "I always did like this house. I suppose I should modernize it, though. I thought about putting central heat in it. That would increase the value of the house." He paused and glanced at her. "Don't you think?"

"Of course - but it would be expensive."

He nodded and lapsed into silence. His financial status was a complete mystery to her. Every Friday they went to town for groceries and he never questioned what she bought. He paid for the supplies with a check and took her and Mary out to eat. He said she deserved the rest and he wanted her to keep in touch with her friends. Why that was so important to him, she wasn't sure, and he never explained.

One thing sure, though. Mary liked him, and the feelings were obviously mutual. He was no more expressive around Mary than anyone else, but he often asked her opinion on things. Mary, on the other hand, was vocal about her opinion of Cade, even to the point of stating that he would be the greatest catch of the century

- no doubt, even an exaggeration in Mary's mind. Yet it left her wondering if Mary was still romantically interested in him. To her amazement, that idea spawned an unwelcome pang of rivalry. Was it possible that he was equally interested in Mary?

"How are things going between you and scruffy?"

His question brought her to the present and she glanced up sharply, warmth crawling up her neck again.

"Scruffy? Oh, he lets me pet him now, but he doesn't want me to pick him up."

He nodded absently as he searched through the mail. He stopped on a small aqua envelope and frowned at the return address.

"Great."

The single word was a combined expression of disgust and distress. She leaned forward and studied the envelope.

"Is something the matter?"

He opened the envelope and read the note, his lips thinning down almost to nonexistence. He tossed the note to her.

"My sister is coming to visit."

She stared at him, shocked by his bitter tone. "I gather you two aren't the best of friends?" She glanced down at the signature.

"Your loving sister, Claudette Cade-Lander." She read the words aloud and he snorted.

"Her visits are nothing more than an inspection tour."

"Inspection of what?"

He pushed his chair away from the table and crossed to the family room doorway. He was silent so long that she decided he wasn't going to answer. As she picked up the dishes and turned toward the sink he finally responded. His voice still had a bitter edge, but there was a touch of musing in it now.

"To make sure I'm not keeping up with the Jones', I suppose." He lounged against the doorway; arms folded across his chest, and contemplated the family room. "Cindy, how would you like to do some redecorating for me?"

She stared at him in surprise. He had never used the nickname – always before it had been Cynthia. Maybe hearing Mary say it so often had burned it into his brain.

"Me?" She asked.

He quirked a brow. "Is there another Cindy in the house?"

"But I don't know anything about...I mean, I don't have any training in interior decorating."

The lip twitched. "You seemed pretty sure of yourself a while ago."

Her face flamed. "I didn't mean to sound like some kind of authority on the subject. I was merely expressing a personal opinion."

He dropped his arms and turned to face her. "Then let me express a personal opinion as well. I think you have impeccable taste. You don't need training - especially not from the people who come up with this fashionable cluttered look. You have a natural instinct for the simple but elegant. For me everything is functional, but you have style."

She stared at him, too surprised to respond immediately. Never in her wildest dreams would she have considered her taste stylish or elegant. Of course, she had never given it much thought, either. She knew what she liked, and it rarely had anything to do with what was in style. But then, he didn't say her taste was stylish - he said it had style. Obviously his taste was compatible with hers. But redecorating the family room? What if he didn't like it after she was done? He was still watching her expectantly.

"I don't know if you realize how expensive it would be. I mean, there would be the cost of drapes, rugs, pictures and other things. I..."

"Make me a list of the things we would need and I'll take you into town. We're not talking over a thousand dollars, are we?"

She shook her head in mute silence.

"Then go ahead."

"But what if you don't like it?"

He sauntered to the stove and poured himself another cup of steaming coffee. "I'll like it." He sipped the hot liquid and winced. "Of course, if you think it would be too much work...you'll only have two weeks."

"No, that should be plenty of time." She moved to the sink and turned on the water. As she watched the sink fill, she considered his proposal - and that other thing. This might be a good time to ask.

"I think it would be a good idea if I moved upstairs." She glanced up as she spoke, and his expression became wary.

"Why? If there was anything going on in this house, it's not like your rooming upstairs would make it look any different."

She caught her breath as the blood lunged painfully up her neck. "I didn't mean that."

It was his turn to color up. "Then what?"

"I meant...Well; sometimes girls are more sensitive about things. I mean, it might be hurtful for your sister to see me using your mothers' things."

The lip twitched again. "There's nothing sensitive about Claudette, but if you want to move into that room upstairs with the balcony, go ahead."

Her face didn't lose its warmth and she gnawed at her lower lip. "What made you single out that room?"

He tucked his hands in his back pockets and shuffled his feet, the color in his face deepening. "I figured..." He shrugged. "I saw you up there one time."

If she thought her face could get no warmer, she was unpleasantly surprised. How often had he watched her sunbathing? It could only have been in the last few weeks since the weather had turned warm. She didn't own a swimsuit, so bra and panties had been her option. The rest of her clothes were there in the room in case he came into the house, and she thought the deck was as private as her bedroom with him out on the range wet nursing his cattle. Apparently she was wrong. She stared down into the sink, feeling violated.

He must have sensed the cause of her sudden withdrawal, and spoke gently.

"I'm sorry. I didn't mean to...I forgot my rope in the barn and had to come back yesterday. I wasn't...I mean I didn't...I looked away."

She glanced up at his tortured face and had to smile. The stoical Russell Cade was stammering around like a school boy. And why? Actually, the bra and panties were far less revealing than a bikini. Was he embarrassed because she was scantily dressed, or because he had inadvertently invaded her privacy?

"It wasn't your fault. If I want to sunbathe, I should buy appropriate clothing." She rinsed a plate and dropped the subject. "I think it would be fun to redecorate the family room. Actually, I haven't had enough to do around here lately."

The extra color was beginning to fade from his face and he turned toward the family room. "When you're done with the dishes, let me know. There is a chest of drawers and a three-quarter bed in the attic. Between the two of us we ought to be able to carry them down to that room." He took a few steps and then paused, glancing back at her. "Feel free to get anything you want out of the attic. I know you'll take care of it." And then he walked away, his shoulders swaying like a pendulum with his stride.

His absence sucked the energy from the room and she stared down at the dishwater. Was Mary right? Was she falling for him? No, it couldn't happen. She wouldn't let it happen. Not when everything else was working out so well. She squeezed her eyes shut and prayed that romantic thoughts would cease to invade her newfound paradise.

CHAPTER FIVE

Cade escorted her to town and purchased everything on the list - plus a few more items. When she reminded him that he was going over the thousand-dollar figure he had thrown out, he merely shrugged.

"It will be worth the investment."

She wondered what would be worth the investment, but didn't want to wind up in the middle of a feud. Was he trying to show his sister up? Impress her? It seemed totally out of character. Nothing Cade did indicated that he gave a hoot about what anyone else thought.

As they packed the last of the items into the back of his truck, he glanced up at her.

"It's early. Let's go by and take a look at your truck while we're in town. If it doesn't look too complicated, maybe I can fix it."

She stared at him. "I...You don't have to do that." He was already responsible for her food and housing. "I can get it towed to a shop."

His eyes held a touch of humor. "You don't want me to interfere?"

"It isn't that. It's just that...well; it's not your responsibility."

"I know. But it would be nice to know you had a way to get out and do things without fear of taking the only vehicle. I know you feel uncomfortable about driving my truck. You haven't used it once."

"Then I'll get mine fixed. I had no idea it was troubling you." Little did he know that she wouldn't have left the ranch if her truck had been available. The ranch was too beautiful - too interesting and too much like home.

He eyed her thoughtfully. "It isn't troubling me, but if you really don't want me messing with it..."

She sighed and shook her head. "You do what you please."

Cade launched into an investigation of the old truck while Cynthia and Mary caught up on the latest gossip. Finally he stepped back from the vehicle and wiped his hands with a rag.

"I think I know what it is. I'm going to go get a part. I'll be back in a few minutes."

Cynthia reached for her purse. "Let me give you some money. How much do you need?"

He lifted a hand and shook his head. "No, I'll get it. If it doesn't work, it's my problem. If it does, then you can pay me back if you want."

"Parts plus labor," she insisted.

He eyed her sternly. "I'm not a mechanic."

She wrinkled her nose at him. "That's a fine thing to be telling me while you're working on my truck."

His eyes twinkled with mirth, but he refused to let the rest of his face respond. Mary stood by, unusually quiet, but when Cade left she found her voice.

"So, can you still tell me you're not romantically interested in him?"

Cynthia rolled her eyes. "Let's not go through this again. Nothing is going on and nothing is going to happen."

Mary shrugged and smiled wryly. "Then why were you flirting with him?"

Cynthia gasped. "Flirting with him? I wasn't flirting with him." She knew her face was getting red. Had she been flirting - unconsciously? A Freudian slip? And more important, did Cade think she was flirting?

Mary contemplated her soberly for a few moments and then spoke gently. "Be careful, Cindy. I know you're sure you can stay in control, but..."

"I can," Cynthia replied archly. "And anyway, Cade definitely isn't romantically interested in me, so there's absolutely nothing to be concerned about." Both statements came from the heart. People had limited control over their emotions, but they could certainly remain in control of their actions.

Mary shrugged. "Well, if I were in your shoes, I'd see my doctor about some form of birth control. People have urges and sometimes things just happen."

"Oh, Mary. The best method of birth control is abstinence and a little pill is no substitute for morality. Anyway, things don't just happen. Not to people who have a little dignity and self control." At Mary's startled look, she was afraid she had stepped over the line. Did Mary speak from experience? It was none of her business and she certainly didn't want to hurt Mary's feelings. "Well, maybe it does for some people, but not a hard hearted old witch like me."

Mary laughed shortly. "You two make a fine pair, you know that? Who do you think you're fooling? Under that facade of indifference beats a heart primed for breaking."

"Maybe so, but not right now. I'm having too much fun." She launched into an explanation of the truckload of supplies and a description of her new room.

Mary listened thoughtfully. "Claudette has no reason to be concerned about Mrs. Cade's furniture. It isn't..." She cut her explanation off short as Cade pulled into the drive. "I'll tell you about it later."

But the opportunity to talk privately didn't offer itself the rest of the day. As it turned out, the truck repair was minor, so she was able to follow Cade home that evening. It would be nice to know she could leave the ranch at will without leaving Cade afoot, but she doubted if she would be driving to town soon. For a while she was going to be far too busy.

The next morning, after Cade left, she threw a roast in the oven and eagerly set to work on the family room. By noon she had the pictures and mirrors on the walls and was hanging the curtains when Cade came in. He glanced around the room and his troubled gaze halted on her.

"Don't over do it."

She glanced around the room anxiously. She was little more than half-done and already he thought it was too much? What was it he found so objectionable? Unable to discern the source of his objection, she finally turned an inquisitive gaze on him.

"You don't like it?"

He actually smiled, though it was so brief that she questioned whether she had imagined it. No, it had been there - brief and beguiling. And now it was gone, not even a trace lingering as he spoke.

"I meant don't over work yourself."

"Oh." She took a step down and missed the next rung - plunging her shin against the step. She gave a startled squeal and fumbled on the unsteady ladder.

Instantly strong arms scooped her off the ladder and lowered her safely to the floor. It all happened so fast that she didn't have time to think, only to cling to the one solid thing she could find - Cade. The arms that rescued her continued to cradle her gently, and what the fall had failed to do to her heart beat, his close proximity completed.

Color raced to her cheeks. What must he be thinking to hold on to her like that? She chanced a glance at his face, but he was contemplating the ladder.

"I'd better get a screwdriver and tighten that ladder before you fall and break your neck."

He glanced down and noted her color with obvious confusion. One arm tightened around her in a light hug. He released her, striding away after a screwdriver.

She stared after him, still perplexed by the hug - a fatherly or brotherly demonstration of fondness - or maybe an expression of relief that she wasn't injured? She rubbed her shin. Not badly, anyway.

Maybe that incident inspired her dream that night. How the dream began, she couldn't remember but she was in his arms and he was gazing down at her, his expression as bland as usual. She lifted her face to receive his kiss and he leaned forward, giving her a fatherly peck on the cheek - and a friendly squeeze. She clutched his sleeve as he turned away.

She woke, her fingers entwined in the sheet, feeling aroused and frustrated. She untangled her fingers from the sheet and punched her pillow. What was it about him that she found so attractive? And why couldn't she force these erotic thoughts from her mind? Nothing but heartache could come of it. Cade was completely uninterested. Even in her dream she knew it, so why the persistent desire? Should she walk away from this job? Could she walk away from it - and Cade? The job would be harder to walk away from than Cade - wouldn't it? Mary was right about one thing. She was falling for Cade. It was time to pack up and get out - as soon as the visit from his sister was over. He could always find another maid and she could go back to the diner.

For the next week, she tried to stay too busy to think about him. In her spare time she read "The Lonely Hills." Elizabeth Cade was a lonely woman - lonely and unhappy. Cynthia closed the book and gazed out the window. Why didn't his mother see the beauty of the ranch? She crossed to the window and stood watching another majestic sunset.

Vaguely she heard Cade close his book and cross the room. He stood beside her and they both watched Mother Nature's display in rapt silence. Finally she spoke.

"It's so beautiful. Don't you think?"

"Yes." Something about his tone made her glance up and she caught him watching her instead of the sunset. He reached out and took one of her curls in his hand. "Just like burnished copper."

She smiled up at him shyly. "I was talking about the sunset."

His eyes crinkled and a smile played at the corners of his mouth. She was flirting with him and he knew it. She could see it in his eyes.

She tugged the curl from his hand and turned to the old piano as a diversion tactic.

"Did your mother play?"

He nodded. "Do you?"

She laughed softly. "Chop sticks."

A brow quirked and he motioned to the bench. "Have a seat. Let's play a duet, then."

She made her way clumsily through one episode and then watched as his long fingers moved gracefully over the keys. The tune was haunting and yet somehow soothing. He coaxed one melody after another from the old piano until finally he folded the lid down.

"That's enough. I don't want to bore you to death. It's getting late."

"I'm not bored, but it is getting late."

"And tomorrow is a long day. I'm trying to get everything caught up so I can spend a little time with Claudette."

"Are you beginning to looking forward to seeing her?"

He shook his head and ran his fingers along the rich top of the piano. "No."

"But she's your sister. You must have had some good times."

"Not really." He stretched. "See you in the morning."

She watched his tall figure move gracefully down the hall, forcing unwelcome warmth to crawl up her neck. Some people lived their entire lives without ever being close to anyone. Maybe he simply wasn't capable of having a relationship deeper than surface friendship. At any rate, it was none of her business. A fact he had made abundantly clear.

When Claudette arrived, the room was finished and the house in order. Cade answered the door and ushered his sister into the family room where Cynthia was doing some last minute dusting. She glanced up as they entered - and then stared.

Claudette was a knockout. She had large brown eyes with thick black lashes and matching hair that was stacked becomingly on top of her head. From her long neck to her slender ankles, Claudette was dainty and feminine. Her rosebud mouth curved into a smile that never reached her eyes. She was attached to the arm of good-looking man wearing a business suit.

Cade made the introductions.

"This is Cynthia Turley. I hired her as a housekeeper a few months ago. Cynthia, this is Claudette Lander and her husband Carl."

Cynthia offered a hand to Carl and he accepted it cordially. "Nice to meet you," he said. "I didn't know Russell had a maid."

Claudette glanced around the room. "It's about time he did something with this old house." Finally her gaze came back to Cynthia. "I assume you're the one responsible for the new look. Nice job."

Cade was standing behind Claudette and her husband. He winked and made the OK hand sign. Obviously the room had passed an important inspection. He picked up the luggage.

"I'll show you where you will sleep while Cynthia gets supper on the table."

Supper was ready and the table set. Cindy carefully laid out the food in an attractive manner and retired to the kitchen. A few minutes later Cade popped his head around the door.

"Is everything ready?"

"Yes. It's all on the table. Go ahead and eat. I'll bring desert in after a little while."

He frowned and stepped into the kitchen. "You're not eating? Are you feeling ill?"

"No. I'll eat later."

He shook his head. "No. You'll eat with us."

"But it wouldn't be proper. I'm the hired help."

He scowled at her. "I don't care. You eat with us. That's an order."

"Yes sir."

"And none of that yes sir stuff, either. I want someone who can contribute intelligent conversation, not grovel at my feet."

She raised her brows. "And so you asked me? Don't you think you're setting yourself up for a disappointment?"

His eyes twinkled and he jabbed a thumb at the dining room. "Save the smart talk for later. Get on in there and set yourself a place - or do I have to do that?"

She wrinkled her nose at him as she brushed by and he tugged playfully at her hair. She quirked a brow and made an exaggerated point of putting her hair back in order, tossing her head pertly and smiling up at him.

Claudette and Carl were waiting patiently in the dining room when Cynthia and Cade entered. Sobering, Cynthia addressed them.

"I'm sorry to keep you waiting. I didn't realize I was supposed to dine with you. Go ahead and take a seat while I set another place."

Ignoring the raised brow that Claudette gave her husband, Cynthia hastily set another place and graciously submitted to improper treatment as Cade helped her with her chair and then seated himself. It was hard to tell whether he was trying to impress his sister or shock her. Somehow the latter seemed more likely with Cade.

During and after supper, conversation seemed to continually migrate back to Cynthia. Were the Landers actually interested in her mundane life, or was there some other reason for their questions? The evening was long and she was grateful when Cade announced he was going to bed.

Once she was certain Cade and his guests were comfortable, she retreated to her room with a book. She wasn't actually tired, but reading was relaxing. Inside the quiet room, the balcony beckoned, so she slid the patio door open and stepped out into the balmy night. She leaned on the banister and breathed deeply of the clean air. Down by the pond, frogs were singing their night songs and the sky was filled with bright stars. Somewhere out on the range a lone wolf called, its eerie howl reminding the intruding humans that they had not yet won. She sighed contentedly. This was heaven on earth. How could it get any better? And then she thought of Cade. A cool breeze touched the warmth of her cheeks. Why couldn't she stop thinking of him that way? What was it about him that attracted her so? No matter how often she asked herself the question, the answer remained elusive. Could it be that his stoic personality was the very thing that kept her interest perked? People always wanted what seemed unobtainable. Was that the case? If he returned her affection, would she grow tired of him?

She turned away from the beauty of the ranch, reminding herself that she had made the decision to leave. How could she stay, feeling as she did about Cade? Sooner or later it would become obvious to Cade himself. And then what would he do - suggest she find attention elsewhere? So many questions and so few answers. She settled into the old rocker and snapped on the lamp. A few chapters would take her mind off Cade.

But it didn't, and even when she slept, she dreamed of him again. This time they were on the balcony, gazing into the night, his arm around her waist. She snuggled against his body, but this time when she lifted her lips for his affection, he laughed.

She woke with a start. She rolled over and punched her pillow. Now that was a good example of her imagination working over time. Cade laughing? Did Cade secretly laugh at the way she flirted with him? The idea brought a rush of heat to her neck. She tossed her head to throw the curls from her face and rolled over in bed. Stop thinking about him. It was that simple. All she had to do was put her mind to it.

The clock ticked away the minutes and she finally sat up and squinted at it - four-thirty. What time would Cade want to get up this morning? She threw back the covers. She might as well shower and dress. She wasn't going to be able to sleep any more.

With her bed made, she crept down the stairs and across the family room floor. A sliver of light under Cade's door suggested he was already awake. She quietly crossed to the kitchen and put some water on the stove for coffee. Scruffy was meowing at the kitchen door. Taking a zip-lock bag of scraps from the refrigerator, she opened the door and stepped out into the cool dawn. Scruffy limped to the bowl and she kneeled beside him.

"Come here, kitty. What's the matter with your foot?"

She lifted the cat to her lap and turned so the light from the doorway would fall on the foot. One of the claws was ripped almost completely out. She shuddered.

"Poor little thing. What happened? Did you get caught in a trap?"

A tall figure darkened the doorway and she looked up to find Cade watching her. He knelt beside her and reached for the cat.

"Let me look at him."

To her surprise, the cat gave him no resistance. Cade examined the claw and stood. "I have some salve in the barn. Let's go put some on it."

"Should we bandage it?"

His features twisted into what might have passed for a wry smile. "Bandages are for humans, not animals - not for things like this, anyway. He'll limp around for a week or so and then he'll be fine."

She smiled up at him. "You like him, don't you?"

He eyed her sourly. "I hate cats."

"Right. That's obvious. "Her smile broadened into a grin as she reached for the cat. "Come on scruffy. Daddy wants to fix your foot."

Cade handed her the cat and cuffed her playfully. She giggled and cuddled the cat close. "He's so soft. Don't you think he's cute?"

"Yeah," he commented dryly as they turned toward the barn. "You've been around that furry thing so long that you're beginning to look like him." He reached out and brushed her hair away from her face. "You're even getting hair in your ears."

She made a face and he smiled. Not a twitch of the mouth or a brief glimpse of teeth, but a regular smile. She caught her breath, realizing for the first time that he was actually an attractive man. How sad that his smile was so rare.

"Do you realize that's the first time I've ever seen you smile? You have a lovely smile, you know that?"

"Get out of here." The smile was replaced by a surge of color as he jerked the barn door open. "Let's get that paw fixed and then go in. I'm about to starve to death."

CHAPTER SIX

By the end of the second day, she had adapted to the guests and felt completely at ease - a state that Claudette apparently wanted to shatter. Cynthia was peeling potatoes when Claudette wandered into the kitchen. Cynthia glanced up and smiled warmly.

"Can I get you something?"

"No. As a matter of fact, you've spoiled us both and we'll never be able to get along with our present housekeeper again."

Cynthia laughed. "Oh, she can't be that bad."

Claudette shrugged. "No, you're just that good."

"Thanks."

Claudette laced her fingers and leaned against the counter, eyeing Cynthia with a puzzled expression.

"You know, I've never seen Russie look so fit. You two seem to get along well together."

"Most of the time."

Claudette arched well maintained brows. "How well?"

Her intent was obvious, but Cynthia decided to play dumb. "Oh, we disagree now and then, but we never come to blows."

Claudette rolled her eyes. "No, that wasn't what I meant." She moved away from the counter. "Of course, what goes on between you two in this big lonely house when no one else is around is between the two of you."

It would be disrespectful of Cade for her to do anything but defend his honor. She rinsed a potato and dropped it in the kettle.

"Mrs. Lander," she began in a cordial tone. "There is nothing going on between Mr. Cade and me that anyone isn't welcome to watch. I am the housekeeper, not his mistress."

Claudette's laugh was short. "Maybe so, but I've seen the way you look at him when you forget yourself. You'd like to be his housekeeper all right - and more, I suspect."

Cynthia didn't dignify her statement with an answer. Any denial would be immediately detected as a lie, anyway. At the moment, it was her honor at stake, not Cade's. She completed peeling another potato and rinsed it before Claudette finally gave up on a response with an audible sigh.

"Well, it doesn't matter anyway, I suppose. Russie is a lost cause. I mean, he isn't interested in women."

Cynthia jerked her head around and stared at Claudette. What kind of comment was that to make about her brother? And what, exactly, did she mean?

Claudette frowned. "Surely you've heard. He likes guys. He's gay."

Confusion flooded Cynthia's mind, drowning her in doubt and questions. Was it possible? No. It didn't fit in with anything Mary had said. And yet, Claudette was his sister. Maybe...no.

"Your brother's sexual preferences are none of my business."

Claudette stared at her. "Russie? He's not my real brother. He's not even a Cade. You mean you didn't know that, either?" She shook her head and clicked her tongue against the top of her mouth. "Russie has been keeping secrets from you. I wonder why?"

Cynthia picked up another potato and eviscerated an eye. "No, I didn't know. And it's none of my business. And

Mr. Cade has done nothing to make me think he is anything but a normal man who simply enjoys his solitude." She felt sick to her stomach. Was it possible that Cade actually was a homosexual? Was it wishful thinking that made her so certain that he wasn't?

Claudette shrugged her lovely shoulders. "Well, he did spend a lot of time with his mother. She was such a strange woman - just like Russie. I never did understand why Dad married her. Did you know she actually spun the wool to knit sweaters? I mean it wasn't like we didn't have the money to buy clothes or anything like that. And that old furniture she brought here. Dad would have given her anything she wanted. He was crazy about her. She hated this house, though. Not that I blame her." She glanced at Cynthia. "Oh, you have it fixed up nice, but don't you think it's a monstrosity?"

"No. As a matter of fact, I think it has character."

"Anyway," Claudette continued. "When Dad died, he left this ranch to his wife and stepson and his fortune went to the rest of us kids." Claudette turned her palms to the air. "As far as I'm concerned, good riddance to the ranch."

Cynthia frowned. "You have other sisters and brothers?"

Claudette nodded. "A brother in Maine and a sister in Washington DC."

The diversion didn't last long. Claudette brushed some lint from the bodice of her dress. "Like I said, Russie's mother was always strange, but after Dad died, she really became eccentric. Locked herself in her room for days working on layette sets for the grand children Russie would never provide. I actually felt a little sorry for her. It was so pathetic. Anyway she finally got so lonely and depressed that she locked herself in her room one day and shot herself. Russie came home that night and found her."

The mental picture of Cade finding his mother that way made Cynthia's stomach lurch uncomfortably. So that was why Cade felt responsible for his mothers' death. How sad. She thought of the layette sets in the chest. Obviously Cade's mother didn't subscribe to the gay story - or was that what finally drove her over the edge? Yet Cade had kept the baby clothes - and the furniture.

Claudette shook her head. "That's when Russie got the ranch." She made a face. "Now he's as strange as his mother was. Hanging on to this place and working it like a cowboy. I don't know why he doesn't he get the proper equipment and run it like a modern ranch. I swear, sometimes I think he's completely against progress."

Cynthia began slicing the potatoes in the pot. "I think this place is beautiful, and apparently the ranch is paying for itself. At any rate, Mr. Cade seems to be happy with his lifestyle. Who are we to suggest that it's wrong?"

"He's such a hermit. Everyone laughs behind his back. It's so embarrassing. Every year I come out here and try to convince him to get with the times, but it's to no avail. I guess he enjoys the privacy of isolation. That way he can do what he wants and who's to know? He doesn't date. Would you believe he covers up with the excuse that he's saving himself for one special girl?" She laughed in a single expulsion of air. "I mean, he's a twenty eight year old man, for heavens' sake. If he hasn't been with a woman, it's probably because he's had other ways of ..." She let her voice trail of suggestively and shrugged again.

Cynthia ran water in the pot. "Why is it virtuous for a woman to practice chastity, and ludicrous for a man? I share his philosophy and no one has accused me of...enjoying the same sex."

Claudette digested the response reflectively and finally lifted her shoulders in a graceful shrug again.

"You defend him because you work for him and you're a loyal employee, but I'll bet you've wondered why he's so unresponsive."

Cynthia didn't answer. It was a loaded statement. If she said he was responsive, Claudette would assume something was going on. If she confirmed that Cade was unresponsive she would be as much as endorsing an ugly rumor. Because Cade was so reclusive and entertained controversial ideas, he was a target for that kind of gossip. But it didn't fit the man she had come to know, and she wasn't about to believe it simply because he hadn't made a pass at her yet. She'd like to give Claudette a piece of her mind, but that would be unprofessional. It was Cade's house and sister. As the hired help, she was supposed to be supportive of Cade without upsetting Claudette.

Claudette dropped the subject and Cynthia thought it would never be brought up again. She was wrong - as usual. The very next day she was straining over the counter to reach behind the stove when Cade came into the kitchen.

"What are you doing?"

She lifted her head. "I dropped the salt shaker behind the stove."

"Here, let me pull out the stove."

She slid off the counter and straightened too quickly. The blood drained from her head, leaving her dizzy and disoriented. She lifted a hand to her head and her knees started to buckle. Instantly a strong arm gripped her around the waist.

"Are you all right?"

She staggered on legs of rubber and he lifted her to the counter, sitting her in front of him.

"Put your head down." He grabbed the towel and turned the cold water on. Lifting the hair off the back of her neck, he applied the cool towel. "Better?"

"I feel stupid," she answered through her hands.

Finally he removed the towel and she straightened cautiously. "I think I'm all right now."

He helped her down, his hands lingering on her waist as he gazed down at her. "Are you sure you're all right. I think you've been working too hard lately."

She laughed nervously, acutely aware of the warmth of his hands through her cotton dress.

"Don't be silly. I was simply hanging upside down too long."

Her heart was pounding hard and warmth invaded her neck. The way he was looking at her - was he going to kiss her?

Unsure what to do with her hands, she rested them on his arms. Through his shirt sleeves she could feel the swell of his biceps and her heart jumped into high gear. A wave of warmth rushed up her neck and broke over her cheeks.

Her blush brought a shy smile to his lips. "You know, Cindy, we could ..."

But he got no farther. Claudette spoke sarcastically from the kitchen doorway.

"Well, well - isn't this cozy."

Cynthia fairly leaped away from Cade, her face flaming.

"It isn't what you think. I..."

"Oh, I believe you," Claudette interrupted flippantly. "Now if you been a male..."

Cade looked as if he'd been slapped. He glared at Claudette and swung around, jerking the range from its cove.

"You can get that salt shaker now, Cynthia."

She moved past him and gingerly felt behind the stove until her fingers closed around the shaker.

"I've got it." She pulled the shaker out and glanced up at Cade.

His face was pale and drawn as he shoved the range back into place. His jaw muscles worked as he spun on one heel and marched to the outside door, slamming it as he left.

Cynthia turned on Claudette. "That was a mean thing to say. Don't you care that you hurt his feelings?"

Claudette laughed. "Russie? He doesn't have any feelings. Haven't you learned that yet?"

Claudette had gone one step too far. Cynthia slammed the shaker on the counter, spraying salt on the floor.

"Everyone has feelings, Claudette, though some people are extremely successful at hiding them. If you knew Mr. Cade nearly as well as you think you do, you would know that he is actually very sensitive."

Claudette shook her head. "You've really got a case on him, haven't you?"

Cynthia clammed up. What was the use? It was best to stay out of the entire thing - if they would only let her. Tomorrow they would be leaving, and it couldn't come fast enough. She turned to the stove to prepare supper and Claudette left the room.

Later, as she was straining the water from the potatoes, Cade wandered in. He took a mug from the cupboard and poured himself a cup of coffee. He leaned against the wall, sipping his coffee silently as he watched her mash the potatoes. It was obvious that he wanted to clear the air, but couldn't decide where to start. Finally he pushed away from the wall and crossed to the table. Glancing into the family room, he turned back to Cynthia.

"I shouldn't let her get to me that way."

Cynthia glanced at him and frowned. "She seems to have so much animosity toward you. Why?"

He shrugged. "Who knows? Wild imagination, listening to too many stories, or maybe because I have the ranch. She doesn't want it, but it irks her to think that it was left to me - the weirdo."

Cynthia smiled. "She can't make up her mind whether you're having an affair with me or hiding something. It kind of leaves you in trouble either way, doesn't it? Like the choice between the devil and the deep blue sea."

He glanced up sharply, his lips thinning down and his face paling. He slammed the mug on the table and stood, crossing the distance between them in two long strides.

He jerked her around and grabbed her shoulders roughly.

"I couldn't care less what Claudette thinks, but let me take the question out of your mind."

His lips crushed down on hers, bruising them as his fingers dug into her shoulders. She pounded his chest with her fists and tried to scream. He released her as suddenly as he had begun the assault. She swung hard and her open hand cracked against his face."

His voice was barely more than a whisper. "Nice touch."

That was when she noticed Claudette standing in the kitchen doorway. So it had all been a show for Claudette.

"Of all the..." Tears stung her eyes as she brought her hand around and struck his other cheek with a ringing blow. How could he betray her trust so utterly - for the sole purpose of proving a point to Claudette?

He grabbed her hand. "That's enough, Cynthia."

A sob tore from her throat. "Not nearly." She jerked her hand free and darted past the wide-eyed Claudette - up the stairs and into the safety of her room. Flinging herself on the bed, she sobbed out the anger and hurt. Why couldn't he have confronted Claudette, instead of acting like a beast? And to think she had trusted him. Didn't he know that his brutal assault proved nothing? Did Cade even know how to be romantic? How she would have welcomed a loving hug or kiss from him. But now he had ruined everything. It was bad enough that his actions warranted her decision to leave, but now she actually feared him.

Someone knocked on her door and she wiped her eyes and blew her nose before responding.

"Who is it?"

"Claudette." The voice was strangely timid.

Cynthia hesitated. Was Claudette here to gloat? If she was, she had picked a poor time. This time there would be no holding back. Claudette was going to get a piece of her mind.

"Come in."

Claudette pushed the door open slowly and demurely made her way across the room. She sat on the edge of the bed, contemplating Cynthia with a compassionate expression.

"I'm sorry. I guess I was wrong about both of you."

She was wrong, all right - and she had no idea how wrong she was. Claudette hadn't interrupted Cade making a pass. In fact, she had been nothing more than a spectator for a convincing role Cade was playing. And worse yet, Cade had thought she was going along with his skit.

Claudette folded her hands in her lap. "If you want to get away from here, I'd hire you. We have a beautiful house and lots of parties. You wouldn't be so lonely there."

It was in her mind to tell Claudette to take a long walk off a short pier, but a cool voice interrupted them at that moment.

"Head hunting, Claudette?" Cade was standing in the doorway, coffee mug in hand.

Claudette stood and smiled down at Cynthia. "I'm serious, Cynthia. If you decide you want to go, you can leave with us tomorrow morning." She brushed past Cade, giving him a stern look as she left the room.

Cade wandered across the room and stared out the patio doors, sipping from the coffee mug. For a long time he simply stood there, and when he finally spoke, his voice was controlled.

"I want to apologize for forcing myself on you and I want to assure you that it will never happen again. I took all my frustration and anger out on you. I was way out of line."

"You didn't have to prove anything to me, you know. I didn't believe Claudette."

He glanced around sharply. "Then you're the only one. People are always willing to believe the worst about others. I'm not sure who started that story, but it floated around here for my last two years of high school. It looks like Claudette is determined to keep it alive."

"So you kissed me in front of her. That way she would know you liked women."

He frowned. "No, I didn't even know Claudette was standing there until you slapped me. Then I wondered if you were putting on a show for her to prove nothing was going on between us." He shook his head. "If the show had been for Claudette, would I have been so rough?"

She tucked her legs under her skirt and gnawed at her lower lip. "Then why *were* you so rough? It was the first time you've ever been anything with me but a perfect gentleman. It frightened me. You're so strong." She threw him an accusing look. "Don't you see what you've done? It's inevitable that two people living in the same house are going to be at odds sometimes, but from now on I'll never feel completely safe. If you'd fired me, or even hit me "

"I'd never hit you." The words were swift and emotional and she had no doubt he spoke the truth. He rubbed his forehead and ran his fingers though his hair until it stood on end. "I know what you mean. I betrayed your trust. And I insulted you by being such a brute. I didn't mean for it to be that way. I was so angry, and

Claudette picked the worst time to..." He shook his head. "I have no excuse. I was wrong and I admit it. I told you. It will never happen again."

Obviously he did realize the consequences of his actions. His anger was unfounded, but she had to accept some of the blame for his method of approach. If she hadn't flirted with him, kissing her probably wouldn't have come to mind. Looking back, her words did sound like a challenge. He moved toward her, his expression far from bland. In fact, tortured would be a better description. Yet when he spoke, his voice was decisive.

"Look, Cynthia. If you think you'd be happier with Claudette, I won't stand in your way, but I want to make it clear that I don't want you to go. You're the best friend I've ever had and things around here could never be the same without you."

She gaped up at him, finally snapping jaws shut. "Best friend? I never knew you thought of me as anything but a housekeeper - an opinionated one at that."

He frowned. "There's nothing wrong with having a different opinion. It only proves you have a mind of your own." He stared down at his coffee with a sour expression. "I've always been a little inept at expressing my feelings."

A little? That was the understatement of the year. Yet, he stood before her, conceding his shortcomings frankly. She smiled up at him. "Practice makes perfect," she quipped.

He stared at her. "Does that mean you're giving me another chance? You're staying?"

She sighed heavily and slid off the bed. "I suppose so." She slipped her shoes on. "I left supper half done. I'd better go finish it."

Linda Louise Rigsbee

CHAPTER SEVEN

Cynthia was careful not to flirt with Cade again, putting on a professional front when he was around. He couldn't have asked for a better housekeeper, but the atmosphere between them had become strained. Why was it so hard to joke with him without flirting? And Cade had become more solemn in the last few weeks, as if he sensed her dilemma and felt uncomfortable as well.

The tension was taking its toll in another way. Nearly a week early on her monthly cycle, she was caught unprepared. The few supplies she had would barely last the night, especially since the flow was unusually heavy. That meant she would have to drive to town tonight, and she wasn't feeling up to it. She sighed as she set out the supper dishes. Oh well, life was full of unpleasantness and this was a minor one.

Cade came through the kitchen door and pitched his hat on the peg. "Smells good. I'm starving."

"Well, sit down then. It's ready."

He washed and bellied up to the table, proving his statement as he delved into the food. Cynthia picked at her food, pushing it around the plate more than anything else. Nothing looked good and she felt feverish. Finally she put down her fork and gave up the pretense.

"What's the matter?" Cade asked. "Are you feeling puny tonight?"

She shrugged. "I was just thinking. I need to go to town for something so I'd better get started. Maybe I can get back before dark."

"Why don't you let me go in and get it for you? I needed some things anyway and I don't mind driving in the dark."

She picked up her plate and scraped the food into a scrap bowl for the cat. "That's all right. It's kind of personal."

"Oh. Well, why don't you go with me then?"

Dark splotches hindered her vision and she paused, planting a hand firmly on the counter for support. Surely she wasn't going to faint. Never in her life had she fainted. The room began to spin, and she grabbed the edge of the sink. Her knees buckled and hit the cabinet. Cade's' chair scraped the floor and his boot heels hit the floor twice before he grabbed her waist. A burning sensation began in her throat and she realized she was going to heave. The back door was too far away for her rubbery legs, and the only alternative was the sink. She leaned over the sink, retching uncontrollably. Suddenly cool hands were pulling her hair back and turning on the water. She coughed, and tears stung her eyes. It wasn't bad enough she had to pitch her cookies in front of him, now she was going to cry. As she dashed the cool water on her face, the strength returned to her legs.

Cade handed her a towel and gently rubbed her back. His expression was openly compassionate as he reached out, drawing her into his arms and guiding her head to his shoulder.

"Why didn't you tell me you were sick? You don't have to wait on me hand and foot, you know." He brushed the hair back from her face and stroked her cheek gently.

She buried her face in his shoulder, hoping he wouldn't notice she was crying. But he wasn't fooled. He patted her shoulder.

"What's the matter, Cindy?"

"Nothing," she managed to respond in a weak voice.

"Then why are you crying? Is it this house? Are you lonely? Do you need to see a doctor?"

"No." His sympathy only made matters worse and she hiccupped.

His voice was anxious. "You're not going to throw up again, are you?" He lifted her chin with two fingers, and the expression on his face might have been amusing under different circumstances.

"No, I feel better now." She said, stepping away from him. She grabbed a tissue from the box on the counter and blew her nose. "I'm sorry. It happened so suddenly that I didn't realize it was coming."

He was still watching her intently. Pulling out a drawer, he removed a paper and pencil.

"Write down what you need and I'll get it. Surely it can't be that personal, and you're in no condition to be going to town."

She stared at the paper. How did she get herself into predicaments like this? She shook her head. "I can go. I feel better now."

He frowned at her suspiciously. "Is it a female thing?"

When she blushed, he nodded. "Write down exactly what you want." When she still hesitated his expression became exasperated. "Come on, Cynthia. We're both adults. There's no reason to feel embarrassed about a normal body function."

"I'm not embarrassed." She grabbed the note pad and wrote a brand name and quantity. "They carry these at the store where we always shop."

He glanced at the paper and nodded. "I know what to get, now you go lay down on the couch until I get back. I don't want you fainting and breaking your neck or something."

"I'm all right. I can go..."

"You can go lay down, like I said." He followed her to the family room and made sure she was safely lying down before he left. "I'll be back as soon as I can."

It was ridiculous - sending him into town after such personal items when she was perfectly capable of going by herself. Of course, if he was already going to the store to get something... A mental picture of Cade shopping for such items brought a smile to her lips. Cade probably wouldn't be the least bit intimidated by the task, though.

Giving him a few minutes to traverse the drive, she got up and went into the kitchen. After she cleaned the table and finished the dishes, she went to her room to get some aspirin. By the time she reached the top of the stairs, tiny flecks of light were dancing across her vision. In her bathroom, she wiped her face with a cold rag and took a couple of aspirin. Pulling back the covers on her bed, she slipped between the cool sheets and let exhaustion take its course.

Cool fingers brushed her cheek lightly and she woke to find Cade leaning over her. The lamp beside her bed was on and he had a sack in one hand.

"Are you feeling any better?"

She rolled on her back and smiled up at him.

"Much."

"Good." He set the sack on the night table. "I'll leave this here for you. "Would you like some ice cream?"

She sat up and grabbed her throbbing head. "I'll come down in a few minutes."

He felt her forehead and rubbed her back. "Headache?" At her nod he stroked her hair. "The ice cream will help."

After he left the room she opened the sack to get her things and smiled. Inside was everything she had ordered - as well as a box of chocolates. Cade knew how to be a friend, even if he didn't know what to say. She put the things in her bathroom and was returning to the bedroom when Cade knocked on her open door.

"Room service." In his hand he held a bowl of ice cream, and his eyes held a welcome spark of humor.

"Oh, Cade," she laughed. "That's so sweet."

He grimaced. "Don't get mushy on me."

He sat on the end of the bed and watched reflectively as she ate the ice cream.

"You know," he finally said. "I think I'll sleep in tomorrow, so don't bother to get up early. I could use a day cleaning up the barn."

She rolled her eyes. "I was out there yesterday when I came back from riding and noticed that the barn was almost as clean as this house. I know what you're up to and thanks for the concern, but I'm fine now." She jabbed the spoon in the ice cream and sighed. "I feel like such a baby."

He frowned. "Why? You've been working for me for almost three months now and this is the first time I've ever seen you sick."

She made a face. "That and the time when I was trying to get the salt shaker from behind the stove."

He shrugged. "That was nothing. It happens to all of us now and then."

She stirred the ice cream until it was soft. "This is good." She threw him a sideways look. "And thanks for the chocolates, too."

He nodded absently and fell silent while she finished the ice cream. He reached for the bowl. "I'll take that back down on my way." He tucked her under the covers as if she were a child. "Now get some rest." He leaned over and kissed her cheek lightly and straightened. For a moment he gazed down at her as though something were troubling him, but he finally turned. "Good night," he said as he snapped off the light. He left the room, pulling the door snugly closed behind him.

Such a strange man. Was he beginning to view her as a ward? Lately his actions were more fatherly than anything else. Maybe he was one of those men who felt they needed to protect and care for all women. Chauvinistic, no doubt, but it was kind of nice to be looked after.

She snuggled down into the covers and yawned. She was warm and Cade was in the house. She felt safe and secure.

The next day Cade worked close to the house - trying to keep an eye on her, no doubt. He was wasting a day because of her. She felt fine. When he came into the house for his fourth cup of coffee before noon she decided to salvage something from the day.

"It's such a beautiful day. Why don't I pack a lunch so we can go down to the pond for a picnic?"

He shrugged. "If you're feeling up to it."

She rolled her eyes. "I'm fine. How many times do I have to tell you?"

He set the coffee mug on the counter. "All right, you pack a lunch and bring a blanket and I'll go get the weed whip and knock down some of the tall grass."

By the time she brought lunch and a blanket down, he had a large area cleared under the cottonwood tree. He took the blanket from her and spread it on the ground. There they knelt and ate their lunch in silence.

A meadowlark pierced the silence with its sharp whistling song. She glanced at Cade.

"You know what would be nice?"

His eyes reflected interest, so she continued.

"Geese."

He snorted. "*Geese?*"

She wrinkled her nose at him. "Yeah, you know. Honk, honk? Can't you just picture them swimming around on that pond, ducking their heads gracefully to feed."

He shook his head. "How about a few chickens instead?"

"On the pond?"

"What's so great about this pond?" He slapped his arm. "All it does is breed mosquitoes and attract snakes."

She glanced around nervously. "Snakes?"

He picked up a piece of straw and leaned his back against the tree, picking his teeth. "There are probably a half dozen of them waiting out there in the grass."

She leaned forward to examine his face, but his expression told her nothing. She sighed and drew her knees up against her chest. "I think you're trying to scare me."

He gazed off across the hills. "You like it here, don't you."

She nodded. "Yes. It's a beautiful ranch."

"You don't mind the loneliness?"

"Solitude," she corrected. "And no, I don't mind. I was raised on a farm, and being an only child, I learned not to depend on others for entertainment."

He stood and walked to the edge of the pond. "You don't miss your friends?"

"I see Mary once a week."

He stooped and selected several rocks. "No boyfriend?" One by one he tossed the rocks into the pond.

She stood and picked up the blanket. "No. I've dated some guys, but..." She paused, folding the blanket. How could she explain in a delicate manner, why she had virtually given up dating? He was watching her intently so she shrugged. "I got tired of being pawed."

He glanced away quickly, his features gaining a rosy color. "You're a nice looking woman. It's only natural that men want to touch you."

She stared at him. Was he including himself in that statement? Was that why he had kissed her that day? No, he said he did it because he was angry. He was merely trying to get her to go out more. Maybe he would like a few evenings to himself and she was always underfoot.

He glanced sharply in the direction of the drive and swore under his breath. Following his gaze, Cynthia saw the little green Ford coming up the drive. Why would he be upset with Mary for paying them a visit? Unless - Maybe he was upset at being caught picnicking with his housekeeper.

In the next few minutes she had reason to believe that wasn't his only cause for concern. Mary strode down the path toward them, a hand shielding the sun from her eyes. She smiled as she reached them.

"You must be feeling better, Cynthia. Russ said you were sick last night."

"Oh, it was nothing."

So Cade had visited Mary last night. Had that been the purpose for his trip to town? Why didn't he simply say he wanted to go see Mary? Cynthia blushed. Were her feelings for Cade so obvious that he had detected them? Was that what their conversation had been about today? He wanted her to look elsewhere for romantic attention. Now his girlfriend had caught them together. It didn't look good for him. She laughed nervously.

"I twisted Cade's arm to get him to come out here with me for a picnic lunch." She picked up the blanket. "I'd better get this stuff back into the house before it's crawling with ants."

With that, she left them alone. Hopefully Mary wouldn't be too angry with him. Mary had never been the jealous type, but then, where love was concerned, people changed.

She had barely finished putting the things away when Mary knocked on the kitchen door.

"Come in. It's open," Cynthia called.

Mary entered the kitchen and frowned. "Why did you go running off like that? Did I interrupt something?"

Cynthia blushed again. "No. We were finished with lunch and having a discussion about the pond."

Mary smiled knowingly. "The pond? Is that all?"

Cynthia shrugged. "No, if you must know, he was trying to encourage me to get out and date. I think he wants me out of the house so he can bring someone home."

Mary quirked a brow. "And that doesn't bother you?"

"No, why should it?"

Mary threw her hands in the air. "Oh yes. I forgot for a minute. There's nothing going on here."

Cynthia frowned. "That's right - nothing but honest work."

Mary shrugged. "Whatever. I came out here to enjoy your company, not argue with you. So, how's scruffy doing?"

Cynthia grabbed the opportunity to change the subject.

"He's a regular pet now. And he's getting as fat as a hog on all the table scraps."

They talked for several hours and when Mary left, Cade was nowhere in sight. Had Mary accused him as well? He came in for supper and ate in silence. After supper he went to his room with a book. The evening was young and she had ruined his chance to spend it with Mary. She had to get out some so he could have a life.

Linda Louise Rigsbee

CHAPTER EIGHT

Over the next couple of weeks, Cynthia made a few visits to town, once taking in a movie before she returned. But if Mary and Cade met, there was no indication. Maybe they were having a fight.

One beautiful day followed another and she gradually wandered farther from the house exploring the ranch - sometimes on horseback, sometimes on foot. It was on one of these occasions that she wandered farther than she realized. A low rumble brought her attention to the horizon. The clouds were low and moving fast. In the distance they were dark and threatening. She turned to go back to the house and realized she wouldn't be able to make it before the storm caught up with her. Her heart in her throat, she raced down the hill. She turned at the drum of hooves behind her and watched Cade plunge his horse down a steep embankment and turn toward her. He rode as if he were part of the horse, his lean body swaying with the stride of the graceful animal. He drew his mount to a halt beside her and kicked one foot free of the stirrup, offering a hand up.

Wasting no time, she jabbed her left foot in the stirrup and lifted her hand to be swallowed in his. He pulled as she lunged up, and as soon as she was settled behind him, he urged the horse into a lope. The storm kicked up dust behind them, but they managed to beat it to the corral. Tiny drops of rain spattered their faces as she took his hand again and dismounted.

She glanced up at him in surprise. Was she imagining things, or did his fingertips actually linger to caress her palm? His solemn features gave no clue.

"Thanks," she said breathlessly, and stepped away from the horse. He touched his hat and turned the horse toward the barn.

Wind and rain slashed at her as she reached the kitchen doorway and she hurried into the house. The chicken was done. She had set it in the oven to stay warm before she left the house. The salad was in the refrigerator and coffee was ready on the stove. She prepared the table and was putting the food on when Cade opened the door. Even his hat was sagging with moisture. His boots sloshed as he tiptoed across the kitchen floor.

"Hold that food while I change."

He returned to the kitchen after a few minutes in dry clothes, his hair freshly combed. She poured him a cup of coffee and sat down at the table.

The storm moved over them as they ate, rumbling and flashing angrily. Cade ignored the uproar and gave proper attention to his meal. Was he going to say something about the fact that she wandered too far from the house? Was he going to wait until later? Finally she could bear the suspense no longer.

"I didn't notice how far I was wandering this evening."

"It can happen to anyone."

He continued to eat, ignoring her presence, and she squirmed in her chair.

"You're not going to lecture me about it?"

He glanced up at her and frowned. "Lecture you? Why? Everything turned out fine and you learned a lesson. What more could I say?"

She smiled at him gratefully. "Behind that facade of indifference, there's a very nice person."

His brows lifted in genuine surprise. "Me?"

She wrinkled her nose at him. "You."

He shrugged nonchalantly, but his gaze rested on her thoughtfully for a few moments before he finished his meal.

The storm passed quickly, but the night remained warm. There was probably another one brewing. It was that time of year. When she crawled into bed and turned off the light, the night sky performed a fireworks display in the distance. She stretched and tried to relax, but her mind kept returning to Cade - thinking of his warm touch on the palm of her hand. Funny how little things like that could stay in a person's thoughts for hours. He was clumsy at expressing verbal emotion and physical emotion was beyond him, but his eyes. She shook her head. It was all wishful thinking. Gradually her eyelids drooped and then she was dreaming again.

She was riding behind Cade, her hands clinging to his lean hips. Lightning flashed around them and thunder rumbled. He leaned forward as he helped her dismount at the barn, rain rolling off the brim of his hat in a stream. His fingers caressed her palm warmly. He brushed the hair away from her cheek. She stood on her toes and stretched upward to kiss his lips. He was leaning down to meet her, but they couldn't seem to touch.

She came awake with a start as thunder rattled the entire house. A stream of rain was splattering on the patio. A bolt of lightning lit up the bedroom. She threw the pillow over her head, drawing the light blanket up against her chin. Her heart was pounding and the storm wasn't the only reason. She shivered in her light cotton nightgown and curled up into a ball. How could it be so cold during an electrical storm? A brilliant flash of lightning was immediately followed by thunder so loud that it rattled the windowpane. A rumble began and it took her a moment to realize the sound was hail pounding on the roof.

She threw the covers back and dashed to the patio doors, staring outside. Hail meant turbulence, and turbulence meant there could be a tornado close. She took a quick step back. If it was a tornado, standing next to glass doors wasn't the smartest thing to do. What was? She wracked her mind for tornado safety rules. Get to the lowest story, in a central location away from hallways and windows. She grabbed her blanket and hurried down stairs. Where was Cade? Was it possible for him to sleep through this weather? As she entered the family room, a warm glow beckoned from the fireplace. A dark form hunkered before the fire, feeding small twigs to the flames.

Her bare feet made no noise as she moved across the room toward him, so when she reached his side he glanced up sharply. He let his breath out slowly.

"You startled me."

"I'm sorry. I was just... well, the storm was so violent, and it was so cold."

He glanced at the blanket. "Make sure you don't get any sparks on that thing." He turned his attention to the fire and tucked another piece of bark into the bright coals. His bare shoulders glistened in the flickering firelight. He wore only pajama bottoms, his feet bare as well.

She clutched the blanket under her chin and shivered. That was when she noticed the chill bumps on his arm. He wasn't about to let on that he was also cold. She scooted closer to him, shifting the blanket so that she could drape the excess around his shoulders.

He glanced at her and declined the blanket. "I'm fine. Why don't you curl up on the couch and get your bare feet off this cold floor?"

Feeling rejected, she nodded and moved to the couch. She sat on her feet and huddled under the blanket, watching the flames grow. Maybe the stories were true. Maybe she and Mary were merely his friends. Maybe that was why Mary seemed so concerned that she would become romantically involved with Cade. It would certainly explain Cade's actions. Was he confused – alone and fighting a desire he detested?

Cade finally left the fire and sat down beside her on the couch. He rubbed his arms, unable to completely suppress a shudder.

"Here," she said, draping the blanket around his shoulders again. "There's no point in being uncomfortable just so you can prove what a macho man you are."

He accepted the blanket with a sour look. "I wasn't trying to play macho man."

She snuggled close, letting his body draw warmth from hers. The storm raged on around them and finally began to abate. Thunder rumbled in the distance and Cade's chin slumped to his chest. Leaning forward, she relinquished the blanket and urged him to lie down on the couch. His fingers gripped her wrist as she started to move away.

"Don't go," he muttered sleepily.

She hesitated. It was a risky thing, lying down on the couch with a man, but this was Cade - half asleep and asking her to stay - Cade, who never asked for anything. Cade who felt no desire for a woman? A few minutes wouldn't hurt, and then he would be sound asleep. She could leave and he would never know the difference. He probably wasn't even awake enough to know who she was.

She stretched out on the couch beside him; resting her head on his chest and he draped the blanket across her shoulders, his arm falling loosely on her waist. Almost immediately his breathing changed and she knew he was asleep. She'd give him a few more minutes to get completely relaxed before she left.

Cynthia was dreaming again. Cade was beside her; resting on one elbow as he stared down at her. He smiled, brushing a strand of hair from her cheek. Only in a dream, she thought sluggishly and reached out to touch his cheek. He turned his head and kissed her fingers. She smiled languidly. He leaned down and kissed her cheek softly and she rolled her head, finally touching his lips briefly with hers.

He drew back, gazing down at her with a perplexed expression. Hesitantly he leaned forward again, softly brushing her lips with his. His lips were warm. She gazed up at him, her heart beginning to flutter. A queasy feeling began in her stomach. Again he bent his head and his lips questioned hers gently at first, and then with more emotion when she responded.

With a start she realized that this was no dream. Cade was actually kissing her - and very well. For a moment she lay still, afraid any movement would frighten him away like a wild cat in the daylight. But they shouldn't be doing this. Not here alone on the couch. She put her hand on his chest with the intention of pushing him away, but the warmth of his muscular chest on her palm was exciting. Instead, her fingers slid across the smooth muscles and up to his neck, drawing his mouth down harder on hers.

He finally drew away. "Cindy?" His voice was husky and bewildered as he gazed down at her.

Now was the time to stop this. She should tell him to let her up. That was simple enough. But no words came from her mouth as she lay there, mesmerized by his ardent expression.

Again he stroked her cheek and bent his head. This time his lips left hers and wandered to her neck, sending her heartbeat into frenzy. His hand moved down her side to her waist and then down to her leg, caressing the back of her knee in a delightful way. He was so gentle, so sweet. Could this actually be Cade? And then he moved over her, his fingers sliding up her arm as it lay beside her head. Lacing his fingers through hers, his palms touched hers – so warm and exciting. His lips became more urgent as they found hers again.

For a moment she had the shocking realization that the situation was out of control. She squirmed to get out from under him, but the movement was misinterpreted. She caught her breath in a startled gasp of pain.

"Russ?"

"Darling," He spoke in a husky whisper. His warm breath quickened against her throat. His lips found hers in an ardent kiss.

In the fog of desire she knew one thing - it was too late to protest. All desire to push him away vanished and she clung to him, lost in the ecstasy of his urgent lovemaking.

Some time later she awoke in his arms. The fire flickered feebly, its passion curbed by time as well. She stared at the fire, shocked by the enormity of what she had done. How could she have allowed this to happen? She should never have lain down on the couch with him. She knew that at the time, so why had she pushed reason aside? Because it was Cade. Not only because she loved him, but also because she trusted him. Had Cade planned to seduce her, or was he also a victim of mislaid trust? After all, she had made the first move, turning her head as he kissed her cheek.

She moved away from him and stared down at his relaxed features. When had he changed from the unattractive older man she met in the diner to the good looking young man who now lay beside her? Was she blinded by love now, or had she merely been unobservant before?

She gently worked her nightgown out from under him, hoping all the while that he wouldn't wake. Who would wake from that sleeping body? The man she made love to last night or the recluse - Cade? Her cheeks burned. How many times had she sworn she would never do that with anyone but her husband? She had been so sure it would never happen with her consent. But Cade hadn't raped her. She had been a willing participant. In her confused state of mind, she had convinced herself that he loved her. But now her head was clear. Cade only wanted one thing - and she had foolishly submitted. For him it was nothing more than a brief episode of pleasure.

Tears spilled down her cheeks as she slipped away from the couch. Cade still slept peacefully - not that he would have cared if she left at this point anyway. A lump was forming in her throat and she was afraid she was going to retch. She hurried to her bathroom.

Half an hour later, her eyes swollen and her chest sore from sobbing, she turned her face up to the warm water in the shower. Clenching her hands together she prayed fervently. "Oh God," she cried softly. "Please let me wake up and find out this was only a dream." But when she opened her eyes, it was no dream. She scrubbed her skin rosy for nearly an hour and finally abandoned the attempt to remove the guilt. She dressed as the sun was sending its first rays through the bathroom window. Time couldn't be turned back. The mistake had been made and she had no choice but to acknowledge it and get on with her life. It wasn't the worst thing that could happen. She stopped at the door and caught her breath. No, certainly not. It could be much worse. But it was only once. She shook her head. That was all it took, providing it was the right time. Was it? She tried to calculate, and the blood pumped in her neck. And this could be exactly the right time.

She jerked the door open. Stop thinking about it. It was too late or too early to do anything about it now. In a few more weeks she could make a routine visit to the doctor. She might be worrying for no reason. After all, even if it was the right time, it didn't mean pregnancy was inevitable.

When she came through the living room the fire was roaring, but Cade was nowhere in sight. For that much she was grateful. Yet, when the smell of bacon lured him to the kitchen, she found herself wishing he would address the subject. Instead he was withdrawn and somber, even picking at his food. Finally he pushed his plate aside and rose from the chair.

"See you tonight," he mumbled as he headed for the door.

"Do you want me to pack you a lunch?"

He clamped his hat on. "No. I don't want anything." Without another word, he left the house.

She stared after him. Would he prefer she wasn't here when he got back tonight? Was he angry with her? After all, if she hadn't turned her head when he kissed her on the cheek, maybe things wouldn't have turned out the same way.

Warmth invaded her cheeks as she thought of something else. Maybe he was afraid she would insist he make an honest woman of her. She slammed the plates into the sink. Well he needn't worry. The last thing she wanted was a reluctant husband. If he wanted to forget it had ever happened, so much the better. It shouldn't have - and it never would again.

Linda Louise Rigsbee

CHAPTER NINE

In the week that followed, they drifted further apart. Their friendship had been destroyed by one night of passion. Their innocence replaced with guilt. Why had they allowed themselves to completely lose control? Had it meant anything at all to Cade, or was it merely a moment of desire? Was it the first time for him? It shouldn't make any difference, but it did. Cade was the man of her dreams, but was Mary the woman of his? Had he given himself to the wrong woman? Was that why he was so remorseful?

She stabbed the spade into the flowerbed and gazed off into the distance. It was such a beautiful ranch, so quiet and secluded. A hawk made a wide swing across the grassland and suddenly dived, jerking up at the last second, its great wings straining as it pumped back into the air with added weight. A rabbit writhed in its claws, screaming in terror.

She shuddered. One moment things could be so tranquil and then the next... She sighed. It depended on how a person looked at it. For the rabbit, it was a bad day. For the hawk and her young, it was a good day.

A shadow fell over her and she turned into the sun, shading her eyes with a gloved hand. Cade was standing over her, a puzzled expression on his face as he contemplated her work.

"What are you doing?"

"Digging up these bulbs. I noticed they were getting crowded. I'm going to move some of them over there." She indicated a cultivated area not far from where she was working. "I hope you don't mind."

He rubbed his jaw and stared absently at the spot. "Not at all." He glanced around. "As a matter of fact, the place could use a little sprucing up."

Was he hinting that she should give more attention to the exterior of the house? She pushed away from the ground stiffly and rubbed at the sore muscles in her back while she surveyed the house. Actually, it could stand a good washing and a paint job, but surely he didn't expect her to do that.

She slapped at a mosquito on her arm and glanced up at him. "I didn't expect you so soon. I'll go in and start supper." She removed her gloves, wondering about the slow flush that was darkening his somber features.

He jabbed his hands in his pockets and looked away.

"You haven't been in to see Mary for a while. Why don't we go out for pizza tonight? We could stop by and pick her up."

"Why don't you go in by yourself?"

He glanced at her sharply and regarded her thoughtfully for a few moments.

"Does friendship mean so little to you that you can toss it aside so easily?"

She stared at him. "Mary and I aren't fighting."

He opened his mouth to speak and then shut it again, shaking his head. He squatted and took some of the freshly dug soil in his hand, crushing the lumps and letting the dust run through his fingers.

If he wanted to see Mary, why did he have to drag her along? Of course, after the other night... She slapped her gloves together to remove some of the mud.

"You don't have to feel obligated to take me everywhere you go. If you want to visit Mary, why don't you go see her?" She turned and headed for the house without waiting for an answer. Her eyes were filling with tears and she didn't want him to see. She jerked the kitchen door open, not realizing he was close until she heard his voice behind her.

"If you're not fighting, why don't you go see her?" He dodged the screen door as it narrowly missed his forehead. "Are you angry with me again?"

"No." She reached for the doorknob and he grabbed her arm.

"I've said something to upset you." It was a statement, not a question.

Her eyes were probably bloodshot and tears were beginning to blur her vision. She averted her face. "I told you. I'm not angry." She tried to sound convincing, but her voice faltered.

"Then why are you crying?" His hand still held her arm captive.

"I'm not crying."

"Then look at me." She could feel his intent gaze on her.

"I don't feel good." She reached for the door with the other hand. "If you want to go into town for pizza, please don't feel obligated to invite me. I'm your housekeeper, remember? I work for you. I'm your employee." She pushed the door open and hurried to the sink. "Would you like some coffee or something?"

He stared at her with a perplexed expression and finally shook his head. "I'm going to go wash up. We'll talk when you cool off and get yourself together."

He strode off into the other room.

She stared after him. Maybe she was reacting emotionally. The best thing to do was to calmly tell him she would rather not go. That would leave him free to go alone. But she didn't want him to go. Nor did she want him to see Mary.

When he returned to the kitchen, she was still staring absently into the refrigerator. She glanced up as he walked across the floor and poured a cup of coffee. He met her gaze.

"You still don't want to go?"

"No, I'm not in the mood. Why don't you go on alone?"

He sipped the hot coffee and lowered the cup, staring down into the dark liquid.

"No, go ahead and fix something if you want. I thought you might like an evening off."

She avoided his eyes by examining the contents of the refrigerator. "We have a lot of left-overs and Scruffy is getting ridiculously fat."

"Left-overs are fine." He swirled the coffee in his cup. "Speaking of Scruffy, have you seen him lately?"

She pulled a couple of bowls out of the refrigerator. "No, but there's nothing odd about a Tom cat wandering off for a few days. He's done it before and I'm sure he'll do it again."

He nodded, setting his cup on the counter. "While you're heating that stuff up, I think I'll go out and lock Princess in the barn. I think she's ready to foal and it looks like a storm is brewing out there."

With that, he exited the kitchen.

She was setting the last bowl on the table when he returned. He came through the door, his hands behind him and a smug look on his face.

"I have some bad news."

She eyed him suspiciously. "What?"

"Scruffy isn't a Tom cat." He pulled his hands from behind his back and held them out to her. Cupped in his hand was a tiny black kitten, its eyes still closed.

She gasped, reaching out to touch the kitten. "Oh, how darling." She glanced up at him. "Is it the only one?"

He shook his head, a wry smile twisting his lips. "Five more."

"Oh my gosh." She delicately plucked the kitten from his hand and cuddled it against her cheek. "It's so soft."

He watched her with an amused expression as she petted the kitten and talked to it. Finally he reached out his hand. "I'd better put it back before Scruffy comes looking for it."

She reluctantly relinquished the kitten and watched him retrace his steps to the barn. He hated cats, but he carried the kitten all the way to the kitchen and back simply to show her one. She smiled wistfully and turned back to the table. Why did he try so hard to cover his feelings?

The kittens were a catalyst to crumbling the walls of tension that had been built between them. Over supper they talked of the expected foal, the ranch, and everything but why they hadn't talked much for the last four days. Finally she cleared the table while he sat back with a cup of coffee. After she washed several dishes, she heard a chair scrape the floor behind her. Cade was beside her, lifting the towel from the hook and a pan from the dish rack.

She caught her breath. "You don't have to do that. That's what you pay me to do. You've worked all day long. Why don't you sit down and rest and I'll bring you a piece of pie."

He lifted a quizzical brow. "You want me to get out of your hair?"

Her cheeks felt warm. "No, I... It's just that I should be doing this."

He nodded, continuing to dry the pan. "What were you doing all day today?"

She grinned. "Not working as hard as you, that's for sure." She made a face at him. "How's that for squirming out of a leading question?"

It was the first time she saw him break down and indulge in a heart felt smile. She gazed up at him, completely disarmed by his smile, and yet somehow proud that she had been the one to put it there.

"All the same," he said, "You're entitled to a little free time yourself. You shouldn't be cooped up with a sour old man every evening."

"You're not old." She caught her breath and glanced up at him with wide eyes. "I'm sorry. You're not sour either."

His mouth twisted into what might have passed for a smile. "Just a little taciturn, huh?" He tucked the pan into the cabinet.

"You don't seem to be very happy. Sometimes I wonder if you..." Her voice trailed off. Why was he looking at her like that?

"If I have any feelings at all?" His eyes were dark and distressed. He reached out, gently slipping a hand behind her neck. His thumb caressed her jaw as he gazed down into her face. "You still wonder, Cindy - Even after the other night?" His voice was soft and husky. He cupped her face in his hands and leaned down, brushing her lips softly with his. His lips were warm and inviting, and she involuntarily responded to their query. If only he would always be this way.

Tenderly, he gripped her shoulders, pulling her close. His hands slid down her back to her waist and stopped, drawing her against his warm body. Her arms slid around his neck of their own volition and she pressed close to him passionately returning his affection.

He lifted her into his arms and turned toward the family room door. She squirmed and he lowered her to the floor. She dodged his arms.

"Cade, I haven't finished the dishes."

He frowned. "You're off the clock now." And with that he swept her into his arms and claimed her lips.

She tried to resist the desire that ransacked her body, but his lips and hands broke down every wall she built - shut off every avenue of escape until she no longer wanted to escape... until she no longer questioned his love. Why resist? What could happen that hadn't already happened? He loved her and she loved him. What was more important?

"Russ." She whispered softly as she slipped her arms around his neck and returned his passionate kiss. He lifted her into his arms and carried her to his bedroom, gently lowering her to the bed. This time there was no hesitation, no rush. Everything was going to be all right now.

But nothing was different when she woke in his arms hours later. Again she had abandoned morality and shamed herself in front of him. Why had she thought he loved her? He was merely devastatingly accomplished at lovemaking - sex. Nothing more. She had allowed herself to fall into the role of mistress. At least he had the decency to remind her she was off the clock and therefore not a whore - or was she?

She slipped from his bed, feeling sick to her stomach. This was the last time. From now on she would tell him to keep his hands to himself. It wasn't his fault. Hadn't she been entirely accommodating? How could he know she had become serious about him? As far as he knew, she made a habit of this kind of activity. Could a man tell when he was her first?

Her one saving grace was the fact that the next morning he didn't act as though nothing had happened. As he sat sipping his coffee after breakfast he glanced at her.

"I missed you this morning."

She searched his face suspiciously but there was no leer in his expression. The statement was simple and honest, and somehow it made her feel better.

"We shouldn't have... We can't let it happen again." she stammered.

"Why?" Again the question was devoid of implication.

"Because it isn't right... I mean... well you being my employer and all. I'm not a ..."

He stood and carried his coffee cup to the sink, pouring out the remains. "I pay you to take care of the house while I'm out working. I guess that makes me your employer." He carefully placed the cup in the sink and ran water into it. "But what we do with our time after work is strictly between the two of us." He lifted his head and met her gaze. "If you don't want to sleep with me, I don't want you to feel obligated to do so to keep your job."

She caught her breath. "Oh, no. It isn't that at all. It's just that... well, it isn't right for two people who aren't..." She stopped. Would he think she was pressuring him into marriage now?

He quirked a brow. "Aren't married?" At her nod he shrugged. "Isn't it a little late to start worrying about that sort of thing?"

"I should have thought about it before, but it's never too late to stop doing something you know is wrong."

He walked across the kitchen and paused at the door. "People should get married because they want to spend the rest of their days together, not because they've already shared a few nights." He lifted his hat from the peg and clamped it on his head and then paused, one hand on the door while he studied her face. Finally he shrugged.

"I'll see you tonight."

She stared at the door after he left. He was making it plain enough. He wasn't interested in marriage and he didn't want her trying to manipulate him into it. At least now she knew where they stood. Tears flooded her eyes and spilled down her cheeks. How could he have been so ardent last night and so thoroughly indifferent this morning? Last night she could have sworn he loved her. Now his only concern was that she had his meal ready when he came home for supper. What a fool she had been. Hadn't Mary warned her? But no, she had been so certain, so naive. Not once, but twice. There would be no third time. Of course, hadn't she said that twice already? The smartest thing for her to do was to pack up and leave. This was a no-win situation.

But instead of packing, she cleaned the house and went for a ride. Bad as the situation was, she still couldn't stand the thought of leaving the ranch. And for what? At least while she was here she could save some money. If she went back to the diner she would be lonely and broke. None of this would have happened if they hadn't been alone in the house. Maybe she could do something about that and help Cade make some money at the same time. She had been reluctant to mention her idea before, but now she was desperate enough to risk his anger.

So, that evening at supper she broached the subject.

"You know Cade; you could make a profit off this ranch other ways than running cattle."

He jerked his head up and regarded her for a moment with a sour expression.

She hesitated, intimidated by his obvious displeasure. But too much was at stake, so she pushed on.

"Have you ever thought of turning this place into a dude ranch? You have the extra bedrooms and..."

"The last thing I want is a half-dozen little brats running around here tearing things up. Adults are bad enough, but when they bring their unruly offspring, it's unbearable." He scowled at her. "Besides, I like coming home to a quiet house every evening."

She picked at her food and finally pushed it away. That left only one thing. She had to leave - the sooner the better. She carried her plate to the sink. Scraping the leftovers into a bowl, she ran water to wash the dishes. Cade brought his dishes to the sink and paused gazing down at her, but she refused to look up.

His hands touched her waist for a moment. He slipped his arms around her from behind and drew her back against his chest.

"Cindy," he whispered, kissing her neck in a way that made her heart dance with excitement.

She stiffened. "Stop it, Cade. Nothing is going to happen - not tonight or any other night."

He dropped his hands and stepped away, frowning down at her. "If it's that important to you, I guess we could try a few guests. But if this is because you're lonely ..."

"I'm not lonely. And having guests here won't make me crawl into bed with you again, either. I wouldn't use you that way."

"I never said..."

"You never said a lot of things," she cut him off shortly.

"You're angry with me again."

"I'm not angry with you. I'm angry with me. I don't know how I got into this situation in the first place. I always swore I'd never..." He didn't want to hear about her moral ethics - especially since she had thrown them all to the dogs anyway. Face it. She was having an affair with her boss. How much lower could she sink? Loving him was no excuse, because even knowing he didn't love her, she still couldn't find the decency to leave. How could she blame him when she had offered no resistance?

He turned to the stove, pouring himself another cup of coffee and leaned against the counter, watching her thoughtfully as he sipped the coffee. Finally he cleared his throat.

"What would it take to make you happy, Cindy? I have a feeling you're getting ready to fly the coop. If you want me to leave you alone, it's done. I never meant to push myself on you in the first place. I thought you were..." He paused, as if searching for a tasteful word.

"Eager? Easy?" She supplied bitterly as she rinsed the last dish and put it into the rack.

"There you go, putting words in my mouth again. I didn't mean that at all." He swirled the coffee in his cup and shifted uncomfortably. "But you did seem to enjoy it."

She jerked the plug out of the sink and dried her hands. "I did." She looked him straight in the eye. "Does that shock you?" She threw the towel on the counter. "Well, it shocks me." She swung around and left the kitchen. It was time to pack. After breakfast tomorrow she would leave. He managed without a housekeeper before she came, and he could get along fine now. Maybe a housekeeper wasn't what he had planned on hiring in the first place.

Linda Louise Rigsbee

CHAPTER TEN

After Cade left the next morning she phoned Mary. She had to have some place to stay until she found another apartment. Hopefully, she could get her job at the diner. Swallowing her pride, she dialed Mary's number.

When Mary answered, Cynthia stammered around about the weather and every other subject she could think of. But Mary wasn't fooled.

"What's the matter, Cindy?"

Cynthia pushed her glasses up the bridge of her nose with an index finger and cleared her throat of that nauseating lump. "I need a place to stay," she finally blurted out.

"You're always welcome here. I told you that." She waited a moment, but curiosity got the better of her. "What happened? Did you get fired? I can't believe that."

"No, he didn't fire me, but I can't stay here any more. Not the way things are."

Mary was silent again for a few moments and when she spoke it was in a controlled voice.

"All right Cindy. Out with it. What happened? Did you two...?" Her voice trailed off suggestively.

Cynthia wiped a tear off her cheek and when she spoke, her voice didn't sound like her own. "You tried to tell me, but I was too arrogant to believe it could happen to me."

In chopped off sentences she explained the situation to Mary. "I don't know how it happened. He was always so... disinterested, and then all of a sudden... " She started to cry. "Oh, Mary. You were right," she sobbed. "It's all my fault. I shouldn't have come out here. I shouldn't have flirted with him. I put the idea in his head. I can't believe I actually... twice. I feel so ashamed. I'm such a hypocrite."

Mary's voice was compassionate. "Don't be so hard on yourself. After all, you were half asleep and thought you were dreaming. Remember, he woke you." Mary sighed. "It's probably the strongest urge you'll ever experience. What's worse, you were so naïve - and you love him."

"But after the first time, I should have known. I did know. I just convinced myself we were going to make it right. I rationalized myself right into his bed - right where I wanted to go. Am I some kind of a nymph? Am I completely lacking in self discipline?"

Mary was silent a long time and then she finally spoke. "Cindy, sleeping with Russ isn't the worst thing that has happened to you. Listen to yourself. You've lost almost all of your self-esteem. You're asking questions I can't answer. They're questions you're going to have to answer for yourself. Maybe it would be a good idea for you to stay out there a while and find the answers."

"Stay here?" Cynthia gasped. "You're the one who told me I shouldn't come out here in the first place. Or is it because now I have nothing to lose?"

"It's because you have everything to lose." Mary answered quickly.

"Every day I stay in this house I degrade myself further. He doesn't want to marry me."

"Why should he? He has everything he could want, without the commitment." She ignored Cynthia's horrified gasp. "Don't look at the past so negatively. You've gained some valuable experience about how things can get out of control so quickly. You can run away from him, stay in the same relationship, or set your foot down and get things back into control. Which way do you think will help you regain your dignity?" A short pause, then: "Of course, it's your decision. You're welcome here no matter what - just pack up and come over. But think about what I said, OK?"

And so it was that Cynthia decided to stay on the ranch. Things returned to normal - almost. Except now there was a strain on their relationship. It was obvious that Cade couldn't understand her sudden change of behavior, but he made no further attempts to seduce her. She couldn't say he was less attentive - on the contrary. Maybe he knew he was about to lose a good housekeeper. Maybe he realized their relationship was immoral. Whatever the case, he kept his distance. That created another problem. If he refrained from making advances, how could she know if she was capable of resisting him? But then, hadn't she already done so when he tried to kiss her at the sink two weeks ago? Had it been that long since she talked to Mary? Tonight she would have to call her - after she and Cade returned from their ride.

This time they started out heading west, into a maze of arroyos and low brush. Occasionally they ran across small herds of cattle and she began to realize how large his ranch actually was. No wonder Cade was gone all the time. She glanced at him as he rode beside her.

"Why don't you drive out here with your truck? You could cover more area that way."

He nodded. "Sometimes I do, but most of the time it's simply impractical. I'd travel so far and then I would be stopped by a gully or a creek. If I didn't bring a horse or something, I'd be afoot from then on."

"But you could put an ATV in the back of your truck."

"I know." They rode in silence for a few minutes and finally he looked up. His lips twisted into a wry smile. "I know people think I'm crazy, but I'd like to keep the ranch as near its natural state as possible. I'm not opposed to technology, I simply enjoy the work." He turned his horse and beckoned for her to follow. "Come here. I'll show you something. I think you're one of the few people who would truly appreciate it."

They rode up a long slope and topped out, overlooking a small fenced-in valley. It was situated in such a way that it collected all the moisture from the hills and appeared to be planted in alfalfa. At one end of the field was a lean-to shelter with some kind of equipment stored under it.

He kicked his horse into motion and she followed him down the hill to the shed. Inside the lean-to was a menagerie of antique farm equipment. All were in excellent condition and she suspected that he probably used them regularly. An old sickle mower and rake with their high metal seats were the only items she recognized. She glanced at him and smiled.

"Horse drawn equipment. I remember seeing some pictures of Granddad on an old rake like that." She dismounted and examined the equipment more closely.

Cade joined her and climbed up into the seat on the sickle. "You use this lever to lower the sickle, like this and then lift it over stumps and such." He went to the rake. "You lower the tines until they touch the ground. When the tines get full of hay, you lift it. If you dump them evenly you have rows of hay. Then you use the old baler to scoop the hay up. You have to tie the bales by hand, though. It gets tedious, but I get a kick out of doing it that way."

She ran her hand over the smooth clean surface of the baler. How did he manage to keep everything in such good condition? Cade was a worker; there was no doubt about that. No wonder he wasn't interested in a wife. He didn't have the time. Yet he had found the time to invite her on this ride. She glanced up again and realized he was waiting for some kind of response. She smiled.

"You keep it all in such fine condition. You obviously appreciate it. Has it always been on the farm?"

"No, I searched a long time before I found each one and I paid dearly. I suppose there are some people who would consider it unthinkable to keep it in operation. Actually, I've had to have some replacement parts specially made."

"I think it's wonderful that you have preserved an old way of life. It's just too bad that you're the only one who gets to enjoy them. You know, Cade, there are others who feel the same way you do about the old ways."

He frowned. "So what do you want me to do, make a museum out of this place? No, I may be selfish, but I don't want a bunch of tourists traipsing around my property."

"I know; you like your solitude." She mounted again and watched him swing lithely into the saddle. "If you opened the place up to tourists, the ranch would lose its purity ...but it seems such a waste." She shrugged. "It's such a big ranch and...well; haven't you ever considered hiring some help?"

He stared out across the field. "Mom always told me I was vain enough to think I was the only one who could do things right. If I had paid more attention to her and spent a little less time out on the range, she might be alive today." He stared at her. "You remind me of her sometimes."

Whether that was a good or bad thing she couldn't guess, and she didn't have time to ask. He turned his mount and started up the hill at a lope. It was difficult enough to stay with him - conversation was impossible.

Again they traveled across the wild country. Several times they scared up a covey of quail and once even a wild pig. As the sun reached its zenith, they put their horses down a steep slope. Below them a creek wound sluggishly through a narrow valley. Was this the same creek they had stopped to eat lunch beside that first time? It was a good thing Cade was with her, because she had no idea how to get back to the house.

At the creek Cade drew up and dismounted. "This looks like a good spot to eat lunch." He lifted his arms to help her down.

After a slight hesitation, she leaned forward and gripped his shoulders. He grasped her waist and lifted her bodily from the saddle. It all appeared innocent until her feet touched the ground, and he pulled her close, wrapping his arms around her as his lips sought hers hungrily. She struggled, but his grip was firm - and then he released her.

She backed away from him, wiping her mouth as she threw him a poisonous look. Had he brought her all the way out here to force himself on her?

He shrugged, turning to his saddlebags for the food. "I thought you might have thawed out a little by now. Obviously I was wrong." He jerked the saddlebags from the back of his horse and glowered at her. "You know, Cindy. It doesn't always have to culminate in sex."

She stared at him. "What?"

"You said you didn't want to sleep with me again and I respect your decision. Does that mean we can't indulge in a little innocent affection now and then?"

She moved away from him and contemplated the creek absently. It might be innocent to him, but it was far from that for her. But he did have a point. The only thing she had been proving lately was that she could successfully avoid him. He wasn't the first man she had kissed and she had never considered herself promiscuous with other men. Had she carried things too far in the opposite direction? She sighed and turned.

"Maybe you're right."

He smiled. "I know I'm right. Now let's eat lunch."

For the next week she cautiously accepted his occasional displays of affection. The ugly feeling was beginning to leave, but there was still that other thing. They were making no progress in their relationship. It was plain that Cade was content with things the way they were, but she wanted more. She wanted a permanent relationship with him - marriage. If that wasn't an option, it was time to leave. But as time progressed, his obvious reluctance to propose marriage presented a far more difficult problem. Mary showed up one morning in time to witness that fact.

Cynthia was spending her third morning hugging the stool when someone knocked on the door. Wiping her face with a cold rag, she composed herself and answered the door.

Mary gasped. "You look terrible. What's the matter? Are you sick?" Realization flooded her face with horror. "You're *not*."

Cynthia nodded. "I'm afraid so. I was hoping I was simply a few weeks late, but it's been over three now and then this started."

"What did Russ say?"

Cynthia dropped to the couch and held the cool rag to her face as a new wave of nausea clutched her stomach. "He doesn't know - and I'm not going to tell him."

Mary gaped at her. "Why not?"

"Because he doesn't want to get married and I'm not going to force him into it by making him feel guilty."

Mary shook her head. "Then what are you going to do?"

Cynthia removed the rag from her face and stared at her friend. "Move out. Do you think I can get a job at the diner again?"

Mary nodded. "Sure. Chet never did hire anyone else. He's still short-handed. You can move in with me. But don't you think you should tell Russ? After all, he has a right to know."

"I know I'll have to tell him eventually, but I'd rather wait until I get a job and an apartment. I'll just write him a note and..."

"A note? For crying out loud, Cindy, he'll be devastated," Mary interrupted. If you'd just tell him about the baby...I can't believe Russ would shirk the responsibility of his own child. He..."

"He doesn't want children and I'm not about to manipulate him with guilt. If he's honestly interested in me, he can come courting the proper way. Otherwise, it's just as well we never see each other again."

"I see. So when do you plan to leave?"

Cynthia clamped the rag to her face again. "As soon as I can get packed. At this rate it may take a week."

"Do you want me to help?"

Cynthia lowered the rag again. "I could use the help."

Between the two of them, they managed to get her things into Mary's truck. Before she left, she took a piece of note paper and wrote a short note:

Mr. Cade:
I'm sorry to leave you like this without proper notice, but I simply couldn't stay any longer. I hope you find someone to take my place soon.
Cynthia.

It was the cowards' way out, but right now she wasn't up to confronting him. It was going to be hard enough to work at the diner, but it was something she was going to have to do. There were more important things to think about at the moment - like how she was going to support a baby on her meager wages. The money she had saved would have to go toward doctor bills now. All her dreams had been dashed - all but one. She had always wanted children - although this wasn't the way she had intended to start.

Inside of a week she started work at the diner. Every morning she crawled out of bed and retched for a while before getting ready for work. A doctor appointment confirmed what she already knew, and that everything was normal - as normal as it could be under the circumstances.

Cade never came to visit - a fact that sent her into a down spiraling depression. For the first three weeks she became tense as it approached 8:00 pm each Friday. After the fourth week she knew he wouldn't be back. She would have to accept the fact that she was on her own with the baby. It was hard enough to make ends meet before she took the job at the ranch. How was she going to feed a baby? She couldn't stay with Mary forever. She was faced with three basic choices: Abortion; raise the child herself; or give the baby up for adoption. Abortion was out of the question as far as she was concerned, and nothing Cade might say would change her mind. That left a choice between raising the child on her own or adopting it out. Much as she wanted the baby, she felt adoption was the best choice. What kind of future could she offer a child? She wanted the best for it - better than what she had. And that left only adoption.

In a state of deep depression, she stopped by the social services office on the way home and picked up some literature and a form. Mary was still out, so she sat down and read the pamphlet. Until now she had been thinking of no one but herself. It was time to grow up and consider the needs of the baby. She placed the form in front of her on the counter and began filling it out. They would have to get Cade's consent, but he would probably be glad to give it. Tears flowed freely as she filled out each blank space. How could she give up the baby? It was a part of Cade. How could anyone love the baby the way she could?

She stopped writing. She was thinking as if she alone were responsible. Cade should accept the responsibility of his actions as well. The baby was half his and he should be sharing equally in its financial needs.

She folded the form and stuck it under the cookie jar. This weekend she would drive out and talk to him. He was a reasonable man and she had never known him to shirk his responsibilities. Still, it disgusted her to think of telling him. She straightened her shoulders. It had to be done sooner or later. She might as well pick the time and the place.

CHAPTER ELEVEN

As the weekend drew nearer, the tension grew. What would Cade say? Would he be angry? Would he insist she have an abortion? Could he?

She wiped a table and turned to take the dishes to the kitchen. A tall lean figure entered the diner and she froze – Cade. Why was he here?

He paused only long enough to locate her, and then made a straight line for her. Her heart was pounding as he stopped in front of her.

"I want to talk to you." His tone was brusque.

She moved around him with the tray. "All right, I get off at nine."

He stepped in front of her and took the tray. "No, now."

"All right, I'll ask for a break." Did he know?

He slammed the tray on the counter and Chet glanced up sharply, eyeing Cade suspiciously.

"Do you need help, Cynthia?"

"No," she answered quickly. "I just need a short break."

Cade shook his head and with a quick move, untied her apron strings. He lifted the apron over her head.

"We're going somewhere else to talk."

"But I can't just..."

"Sure you can." He wadded the apron into a ball.

"Cade, I'm trying to do my job, you can't just march into a person's life and disrupt it and then..."

Her words trailed off at his raised brows.

"Hold that thought," He pitched the apron at Chet. "Go get your own girl and leave mine alone."

"Cade!" Was he drunk?

"Russ," He corrected as he gripped her arm and led her to the door. "Why is it that you can only remember my first name when we're making love?"

His voice was low and she was sure no one else heard, but her face burned furiously. What had gotten into him?

He led her to his truck and opened the door, helping her into the truck. He slammed the door and strode purposefully around to the other side, jerking the driver's side door open. If she had felt the least bit threatened, it would have been easy enough to jump out of the truck. But in spite of his aggressive behavior, she felt safe with him. He obviously had something definite on his mind. And why had he told Chet that she was his girl?

He parked the truck in front of the courthouse and turned to her, dragging a paper from his pocket.

"Explain this - if you can."

She unfolded the paper and gasped. "How did you get this?" And then she saw the note clipped to the adoption form. The familiar scrawl belonged to Mary.

"Thought you should know."

She glanced up at him, her face burning again. Did he feel obligated to marry her now?

He watched her intently, his expression injured.

"Why, Cindy? Didn't you think I had the right to know?"

She swallowed hard. "I was going to come out this weekend and talk to you. I knew you didn't want children."

His brows shot up. "And how did you determine that?"

"You said you didn't want any little brats tearing your house up."

He rolled his eyes "I wasn't talking about *my* children. I was talking about other people's children. Mine will be taught to mind."

She gnawed on her lower lip. "I didn't want you to think you had to marry me. You don't, you know. I can raise the baby..."

"*Have* to marry you?" He shook his head in disbelief. "I tried to ask you more than once, but someone was always interrupting and throwing a new kink in my plans. Remember when Claudette interrupted us in the kitchen? The moment was so perfect - and then she walked in and said that... ruined everything. I could have wrung her neck." He shook his head, obviously still distraught by the mere thought of it. "And you jumped right in and assured her things weren't as they appeared. All that wasn't bad enough, but she had to drag up that old rumor – and I thought you believed it."

She stared at him. "You were going to propose?"

He nodded. "Remember the picnic beside the pond? You know, when Mary put in her untimely appearance. Not that I was having much luck, anyway. Every time I found a way to lead into it, you came up with something else. Then when Mary arrived, you ran off. At the time I thought it was another diversionary tactic. Why did you do that?"

"I thought you were upset because Mary caught us together. I mean, you did visit her the night before, and I thought maybe you two were..."

"Mary and me?" He shook his head. "I stopped by to see her on my way to the store. I wanted to know what I could do to help you. You weren't giving me much information." He frowned. "So that's why you acted so cool for a while."

She folded her hands in her lap and stared at them. Until now she would have sworn that he was the one who never expressed his feelings. Obviously they were both guilty. Now was the time to clear the air, and there was one thing about all this that didn't make sense.

"If you were trying to ask me to marry you, why did you act that way after we..." It was still hard to accept what they had done. She wrung her hands. "Spent the night on the couch," she concluded in a mumble. "I thought you didn't respect me any more."

He touched her arm. "Cindy," he spoke gently. "I've always respected you." He lifted her chin with a curled index finger and forced her to meet his solemn gaze. "I swear, I never intended for things to go that far. I thought I could control my emotions. I always have before. But when you kissed me, something snapped inside. It was my fault. I knew I was losing control and I should have stopped then. To be perfectly honest, at that point, I didn't want to."

She gazed up into his face. "Why should you? I was completely submissive. I thought there was no situation I couldn't handle outside of rape - and I didn't believe you would do that." She shook her head in amazement. "It wasn't that I didn't know when things started getting out of control. It's just that...well, after that, it all happened so fast."

He colored and looked away, dropping his hand.

"I'm sorry. I guess we both lacked experience. I didn't mean to hurt you. When I heard you crying in the bathroom..." He brushed a crumb from the seat and cleared his throat. "I knew I had ruined everything between us. I felt sick to my stomach."

She stared at him. "I wanted you to say something - anything. Instead, you acted like you wanted to forget the whole thing."

They were both silent for a few moments, remembering that emotion packed morning - and another one. "Russ?" His name came easily to her lips this time.

He glanced up. "Yes?"

"If you wanted to marry me, why did you tell me you only wanted to spend a few nights with me? Don't you know how bad that hurt?"

He stared at her blankly. "I never said that."

"Yes you did. You said marriage was for people who wanted to spend a lifetime together, not a few nights."

His face was a road map of emotion, traveling from puzzled, to comprehensive and then on to frustration. He grimaced.

"I can see right now that I'm going to have to be more explicit when I talk to you. If you'll think back, my message was that spending a few nights together wasn't a good reason to get married. I wanted you to tell me that wasn't your sole reason for wanting to get married. When you didn't answer, I thought maybe it was your only reason and you thought better of it."

She reached out and touched his cheek. "Which made three times you were broaching the subject of matrimony and I thwarted your attempts. I must have been driving you crazy. I guess that's what you meant in the diner when you told me to hold that thought."

"Exactly." His hand covered hers and he took it in his, kissing it tenderly. "The worst of it was when I got that adoption form in the mail today. I called Mary to see if you were there and she filled me in on the whole thing." His expression was a fifty-fifty mixture of pain and anger. "How could you think I would turn away my own child? What kind of monster do you think I am?"

"Oh, Russ," she forced the words through constricted vocal cords. "I knew you would take the responsibility, even if you didn't want the baby. That's why I had so much trouble telling you." She stared down at the seat. "I got so depressed when you never called, and I started imagining all sorts of things. Then I started worrying about how I was going to take care of the baby and how much it would miss because I didn't have the money to..."

She swallowed a lump in her throat. "So I got to thinking about adoption. I knew I'd have to talk to you about it sooner or later, but I didn't want to hold the financial burden of an unplanned pregnancy over your head like a club. Nor did I want you to feel obligated to marry me to save my honor. I couldn't give the baby up, either. That's why I never finished the form. I decided to talk to you this weekend, but I guess Mary found the form and took it upon herself to mail it to you." She glanced up and met his intent gaze. "I'm sorry. That's a terrible way to find out."

"Don't blame Mary. I'm glad she cared enough to interfere. No telling how long we'd have continued this crazy sidestepping dance - even if you had shown up this weekend. I thought you decided you couldn't live with the loneliness on the ranch because I was gone so much. I thought maybe that was what you were trying to tell me that day at the hay field." He gripped her hand and pulled her close. "I didn't want to lose you, but I didn't want you to be unhappy like mother either. I actually considered selling the ranch." His hand stroked her hair. "If you'd only said something - told me how you felt. Cindy, our baby wouldn't be a burden to me even if my financial status was shaky - and it isn't. I want this baby. I want you. I love you. Don't you know that?"

A tear slipped down her cheek. "Not until now."

He wiped the tear away with a thumb and opened the glove compartment. Pulling out a tissue he handed it to her. "Here, get yourself together and we'll go in and get a marriage license."

She caught her breath. "Right now?"

He popped the glove compartment shut and stared at her. "Do you have some reason you want to put it off for a while?"

She smiled through her tears. "No." She wiped her eyes. "But tell me something. When you offered me a job, were you thinking of me in any way other than a housekeeper?"

He colored slightly. "I noticed you were a good looking woman, if that's what you mean. But it was a good hot meal that brought me into the diner the first time. It was the meal and a friendly waitress that brought me back. After that I got to thinking how nice it would be if I had someone to cook me a meal every day. One thing led to another and I finally worked up the courage to offer you the job." He shrugged. "I'm not sure exactly when I started falling in love with you. I guess it happened gradually. Little things like the way you took in that stupid cat. And the way you faced everything with a smile. Even the way you felt about that attic. I knew, because I felt the same way. And then that day we rode together. I could tell you saw the ranch the same way I did." He frowned at her hand. "I never told anyone, but I avoided getting involved with any woman because of what happened to Mom. The loneliness drove her mad. I should have moved away, but I couldn't stand to leave the ranch."

"But Russ, she could have moved away. You weren't responsible for her state of mental health. Obviously she was the dependent type or she wouldn't have stayed out there."

He nodded. "I know. I wanted a wife and children, but I didn't want to risk losing them because of the ranch. I suppose if I had met a woman and loved her enough, I would have given up the ranch, but I knew I would be resentful, so I simply avoided any situation that might end up in romance."

"So you hired a housekeeper with a professional attitude." Her smile was wry. "It must have nearly scared you to death when I started flirting with you."

Color returned to his cheeks. "On the contrary, I was flattered. Anyway, it seemed like innocent flirtation." He stared absently out the window and continued. "Then we took that ride and you were so impressed with the country. That's when it first crossed my mind that you might be the one." He took a deep breath and turned to her again. "Then the day you fell on the ladder and I caught you - I figured you suspected then." He paused and lifted a brow.

It was her turn to blush as she recalled the dream that episode had inspired. "Maybe I did, subconsciously. I think it was a turning point for me, too. I thought you were going to..." Her face grew warmer.

He smiled. "Kiss you? I thought about it, but I was afraid you'd get mad. Anyway, I was doing my best not to let things get out of control. You can't believe how many cold showers I've taken."

She bit her lower lip and looked down at her hands again. All this time she thought she was the only one with the torrid thoughts.

He chuckled and ran cool fingers across her hot cheek. "By the time Claudette showed up, I knew for sure. She must have suspected as well. That's when I decided to ask you to marry me." He shrugged. "The rest you already know."

"About the courtship of the recluse?" She leaned toward him and he met her half way. Their kiss was warm and exciting - deeply gratifying. Still, his next words were the most gratifying of all.

"Let's get married as soon as we can. The house has been unbearably lonely without you."

Russell Cade - the recluse - was lonely without her.

EPILOGUE

Cynthia spotted him as he crossed the living room and started down the hall, his boot heels clicking sharply on the hardwood floor. She dashed on bare feet to intercept him, snaring him with an index finger in the back of his belt. He stopped abruptly and turned, his expression clearly startled until he realized it was her. His face softened into a smile that invaded his eyes.

"Hey."

She put a finger to her lips "Sh-h-h"

He slipped an arm around her waist as she came up beside him and whispered. "Is he asleep?"

She nodded, hugging his lean waist until they had to let go at the bedroom door.

Together, they tiptoed across the hardwood floor and stood proudly looking down Zach.

"Zachary Russell Cade," he said softly with wonder for what must have been the hundredth time.

Zach stirred and yawned, the tiny hands opening in a stretch. His arms barely reached his ears.

Cade kneeled beside the cradle and touched a blue crocheted bootie. "What's this?"

"I hope you don't mind. I thought she would have wanted him to wear them."

He glanced up at her, his expression unreadable. "I suppose so."

Zach squirmed and made soft baby noises. Cade gently slipped his hands under the infant and lifted him as

129

though he were made of parchment paper. For a moment he held Zach, body in one hand and head cradled in the other. His features softened as he gazed down at the tiny form. "I wish she could have seen this." As he continued to watch Zach, his expression molded into unmistakable awe.

Zach jerked suddenly, knocking his cap off and exposing a scalp full of red hair. Cade looked up at Cynthia, his expression alarmed. "What did I do?"

Cynthia reached down and pulled the cap back on his head. "He does that every once in a while. He doesn't have complete control of his muscles yet."

Cade stood, gently tucking Zack into the crook of his arm. Zach snuggled against him, turning his head and opening his tiny mouth in search of food.

"Here now." Cade's tone was a little startled and a lot amused. He turned to Cynthia, awkwardly shifting him around so she could take him. "I think he's hungry."

Cynthia gathered him into her arms and sat down on the bed. Cade watched as she unbuttoned her blouse and began feeding him.

"Your lunch is on the table," she said.

"I know. I saw it." He made no move to leave.

"I think it's about time to move him from his cradle to his crib." She mused.

"What's the hurry?" His tone sounded a little alarmed, and she glanced up at him. His expression was bland.

"Well, he's about to outgrow the cradle. It doesn't take long." She sighed. Don't worry. I have the baby monitor. We'll hear him the same as when he's in here, but he won't be disturbed by us when we talk."

He met her gaze and his eyes warmed, his lips giving in to a smile.

"You've had the nursery ready for him a long time."

True. They had moved the antique furniture out of her old downstairs room and put it upstairs months before he was born. Together they had redecorated the room and changed it into a nursery. Claudette had sent them so many clothes. It was amazing how a baby could put love in so many hearts. Cade and Claudette might never be close, but they had certainly reduced the gap.

"Oh, I forgot to tell you," he said. "I have a man coming out here tomorrow for the job. I thought he could stay in one of the rooms upstairs at night — if you don't mind."

She caught her breath and glanced up at him again. "You're actually getting help?"

He lifted a brow. "Yes, and I ordered a computer for you too. Dial-up internet will be slow, but at least you'll be able to stay in contact with the rest of the world."

It would be handy when she studied to home school too. Cade was an excellent provider. Who would have guessed two years ago that he would become a happily married man? His smile came slow now, but it came more frequently. Words of praise came more easily to his lips, but he still had trouble accepting praise. He had a gentle temperament, though. Throughout a difficult pregnancy, he had never raised his voice once. The real surprise came with his presence in the delivery room. Who would have thought he would actually clip the umbilical cord? It was strange how he could blush at praise, but watch with unabashed interest while she nursed their child.

Zach was asleep again, so she put him in his cradle and closed her blouse. She stood.

"Let's go eat before it gets cold."

He followed her out of the room, guiding her through the door with a light touch on her waist. He pulled the door shut gently and tiptoed down the hall after her. The way he touched her; the way he looked at her across the room - all those little things were his subtle way of saying he loved her without voicing the words. Maybe he would always be that way. Maybe that was what she found so intriguing about him. Once she had been unaware of his love, but now she had learned to read the signs. He was a man who said little, but felt a lot. In many ways he was still a recluse, but he wasn't wrapped up in himself. They had the ranch and each other, and now they had Zach. They would all grow strong leaning on each other.

ABOUT THE AUTHOR

Linda Louise Rigsbee is a multi-genre writer. Best known for her clean romance novels, she also writes westerns, young adult, children and non-fiction. Linda has published over 30 books and frequently is working on more than one book at a time. Linda writes in story lengths flash fiction, short stories, novellas and novels.

Courtship of the recluse was one of those books that forces itself on an author. The words seem to come from a voice inside and the author merely writes them down.

For more information about Linda Louise Rigsbee and her books, visit her website at www.lindarigsbee.com

Made in the USA
Las Vegas, NV
30 May 2021